K.J.HERITAGE

INTERNATIONAL BESTSELLING AUTHOR

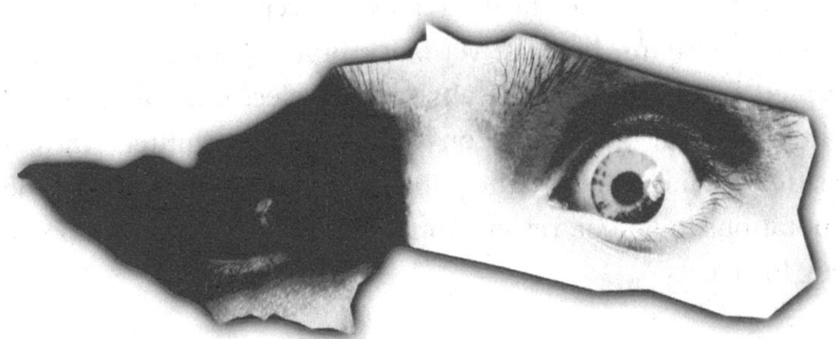

SHATTERED
WEB

For all the trapped

contents

coffin

PRESSURE PULLING at me, flinging me up and down, straining against my arms, legs and back. Spinning me around. I'm trapped, unable to move—like I'm tied to the mast of a ship in a raging sea.

What the hell?

I sense my consciousness returning, a light slowly growing in the distance. This is not waking up—I've been drugged. A powerful sedative is squatting in my system—I sense it as a cloying, swirling cloud. I focus my awakening mind upon the narcotic, directing it towards my liver, increasing my metabolism and sifting the offending chemical from my blood. Finally, I'm able to force back the shroud of darkness and open my one remaining eye.

I find myself in a long, coffin-like box. But this is no burial, I recognise it for what it is… *a one-man escape pod*. I'm wearing my skinsuit, my breath magnified by a flimsy helmet.

Everything is fuzzy. Whatever narcotic has been used on me has temporarily affected my memory.

I twist around, releasing my arms, and I'm hit with

a fresh burst of gees. The pod is on autopilot and struggling. I bring up the HUD and, within seconds, I've got the craft under control.

I pass my eye over the readouts and baulk at what I see. I'm in hyperspace—no one launches a pod outside of normal space, not unless you have a death wish. The conclusion is a simple one—someone wanted to get rid of me. I've been drugged, placed in a pod and forcibly jettisoned.

A beep on the com and a familiar voice. *"Judging by the way that pod is handling, you must be awake. Good, I was getting worried."*

A name slams into my frontal cortex. *Stranng.* And with that name, my memories come flooding back. The Company. Being snatched from my colony ship. The Zeta Karst labs and that goddamn lunatic, Frederix.

"What the hell did you do to me?" The answer flashes into my mind almost immediately. *Shereena.* The ship's over-qualified medic. She arrived at my quarters earlier—a smile on her face. I'd been too much of a sap to bother reading her. That's what you get when you trust someone. And, of course, I'm cursed with vanity. I was consumed by nervousness and excitement—who doesn't feel like that before climbing into bed with someone new? We were kissing and… she stuck a damn needle in my neck.

"I'm sorry," Stranng continues.

I'm not physically close enough to read his intent but I know the man well enough to realise he doesn't mean it.

"Orders from above. Some damn Company grandee,

even higher than your pay grade. Seems like they know what a son-of-a-bitch you are. That's why we drugged you. To make sure you complied. I can't say I was unhappy to get out of that airlock you imprisoned me in. Nor to get you off my ship."

I'm used to tight spaces... who isn't? Even the literal ones like the one I'm presently in. Ship and habitat living is mostly cramped, but I've suffered worse. All due to those damn internment camps I was forced to grow up in—before the Company and its rivals decided to ignore Earth's *Decree of Genetic Manipulation.* 'Internment Camp' was a pretty phrase for *prison*—and not that pretty. Where I spent my formative years with the other Skilled. Punishment for minor infringements was draconian. I spent days in the choky, a box hardly bigger than the ship I'm flying in. It made no difference that we were only kids, although I preferred it in there. To me it was a goddamn reward. I've always preferred my own company. No wonder I got into trouble so often.

"If the Company wants me dead, why not just kill me?"

"That's the point," Stranng replies. *"The Company needs you to be very much alive. Although I don't rate your chances."*

I take in the information with little emotion. "Okay, give it to me straight. Why am I in this flying coffin?"

"Because only small ships can manoeuvre in hyperspace without breaking up. It's taken all my skill to get you this close. Everything was primed and operational in your pod before we booted you off the ship."

"Close to what?"

"You're to dock with another vessel."

"In hyperspace? Are you insane?" The only reply is static. "What damn vessel?"

"Widen your nav-beams."

I do as he says, and I'm surprised to spot a blurred, fluid outline like an extended blob. All com-signals are compromised in hyperspace, yet I can tell it's a design I've never seen before. Smaller and compact. I'm closing in on it fast.

"That's Ariadne. Some kind of experimental warship." Strann g explains. *"The fore-runner for a new fleet. Or so they hoped. The ship cut all coms and launched itself into hyperspace an hour ago and refused every attempt to contact her. Space knows what's happening on board. But we received this message…"*

There's a crackle over the com and then I hear the tell-tale emergency call-sign of a vessel in trouble:

> *Mayday! Mayday! Mayday! This is the CS Ariadne. Urgent assistance needed. The ship has locked us out of all systems. Repeat. We are locked out of all navigational and control systems. Additional. Unknown agencies aboard have shot and killed—*

"Is that all? I don't get it. The ship locked out the crew? How?"

"Ariadne is a bioship. An organic computer is running the show over there."

"You mean they're playing around with biocomputing? That's supposed to be illegal."

"'Supposed' goes a long way with the Company. You Skilled were illegal once, remember?"

I laugh through gritted teeth. A bio-computer can mean only one thing—the goal for computer consciousness is still alive and the Company has only gone and put one in charge of a goddamn warship. Nice. And if you're gonna build an organic computer intelligence, look no further than the human brain. The only problem? *Humans are not that reliable.* It sounds like another mess of the Company's making, a mess that I'm not motivated to solve.

"And here's the rub…" Stranng continues. *"The Ariadne is heading for rival company space."*

I know the Company inside and out. There's no way they'd let one of their ships cross into competing territory. Especially something experimental with a cash value to the opposition. It's that which concerns the Company grandees who put me in this position. "I guess your orders are to destroy the ship before she crosses over to the enemy, yeah?"

"You've got just under two and a half hours, otherwise it's boom-boom time."

"What the hell am I supposed to do over there? I'm only one guy, even if I am a Skilled."

"I'm sure you'll figure something out. Your type always does. Perhaps they want you to talk the ship down? Who knows or cares? I just follow orders. I'm also to warn you that there may be rival agents aboard or even terrorists."

"Terrorists?"

"The Company has tried to keep what I'm about to tell you hush-hush. There's been a spate of high-profile

assassinations over the last few months. Grandees and VIPs. Some say there's a new terrorist group responsible for what's been happening. They call themselves Neo-Dawn. And, as it happens, there was a VIP event on board the Ariadne before this ass-mess kicked off, so watch yourself over there. It's either a malfunction, sabotage or a full-out hijack. Either way, you've one job and one job only. Stop the damn ship and pull it out of hyperspace." Stranng laughs down the com. It ain't a pretty sound.

"And what if I refuse?"

"You don't exactly have a choice."

"How did I know you were gonna say that? The Company must be desperate. The chances of successfully docking a ship in hyperspace are—"

"You're the resourceful type… so I'm upping your odds to one in ten."

"That optimistic huh?"

"I've never heard of it being done before and no skin off my nose either way. You'll find a programmed wafer stuffed down your skinsuit. See it as a goodbye gift."

"You're all heart."

"Remember, you've just under two and a half hours to get the job done. Midnight, ship's time. Or thereabouts. I'll leave it to the last second—you have my word on that. But you've got a bigger problem. You must first dock with the Ariadne to get aboard. Another reason why the Company chose a Skilled—a mere human wouldn't stand a chance."

"It's always nice to be wanted. Anything else?"

"Nothing much. The wafer also comes with a complete ship's roster. There's forty-three souls aboard."

"And that's it?"

"Maybe the Company isn't comfortable sending you any

more info. Or maybe that's all they could manage in the time frame. Make the best of it. You'll be passing out of com range any moment. You'll be on your own." A pause. *"Good luck.... You're gonna need—"* A crackle and Stranng is gone.

"Thanks."

I take a look at the navicom. The blob of the bioship is getting nearer. I'll have to fly in close using sight rather than instrumentation. Stranng wasn't kidding when he gave me a one in ten chance. These pods are difficult enough to manoeuvre in normal space. I'm not sure my piloting skills will be up to the task. Luckily, I'm a whizz on the stick. If I'm gonna survive, I'll need a big slice of luck. I decide to shorten the odds. I increase blood flow to brain and hands and, immediately, I can hear the reassuring thump of my heart in my ears.

All ships in hyperspace create a wake around them, like the disturbed air behind any atmospheric vehicle but significantly worse. The closer I get to the *Ariadne,* the more wake I will experience from her. Any fluctuation that I can't account for will send me careening away—or even kick me back into regular space. Either way, my pod will break up instantly...

My fingers dance over the primitive control panel— making constant adjustments and realignments. I boost the engines and gently edge closer to my target, bringing up the pod's external camera and I see the *Ariadne* for the first time.

Stranng was right. She ain't a normal looking ship. The Company is all about cheap, mass-produced modules. Different components bolted together with no thought for aesthetics. The *Ariadne* is curved and stylish, although I'm too close to see all of her. The Snag Drive array is what surprises me the most. It spreads out from the *Ariadne* like the legs of a spider. I've seen this configuration before. It's not normally used on military ships. The array is too vulnerable to attack, although it's fast and the most stable design for hyperspace. I have no time for contemplation. No matter how pleasing she looks, the *Ariadne* is creating quite a wake. With no schematics, I'm blind—her docking bay could be anywhere. I slow my speed, allowing the *Ariadne* to pull my pod along behind her and, using only the view from the distorted camera feed, I search the smooth, elegantly proportioned ship for a way inside.

And there it is. The cargo dock. A small opening in her stern.

My heart lurches and I have to concentrate hard to reduce its insistent beating. Flying this close to a ship in hyperspace is akin to suicide. The only chance I have is to line up the pod, hit the engines hard and try to punch my way through *Ariadne's* swirling wake.

And if I should make it?

How in space am I gonna stop from crashing? Whether I get inside the cargo dock or not, this ain't gonna be pretty.

I work quickly with the navicom, superimposing the lines of the hyperspatial wake over the crackling camera feed. They ebb and flow—like storm waves slamming into a rocky cove. Every now and then there's a lull. A repeating pattern. It's what I'm looking for. I watch and wait, knowing I've only got one shot at this. I must hope my prediction of the next lull is correct.

My heart wants to beat faster again. This time I let it thump away, sending a signal to my adrenal glands to flood my bloodstream with the adrenaline I'm gonna need to make those precise, speedy manoeuvres. The last wave in the repeating cycle swirls through hyperspace and I punch the engines. I'm slammed by many gees, the adrenaline giving me the energy and the power to keep my hands over the controls, while the *Ariadne* grows on the screen.

The docking bay is only a couple of hundred feet away.

I'm gonna bloody well make it.

I wait to the very last moment. The pod enters the bay and I hit the reverse thrusters, slamming me with even more gee. Lights swirl in front of me. I push more oxygen and blood into my brain and try to steer the pod to a stop.

Shit!

I'm going too fast. The inner hull of the *Ariadne* flies towards me and I smash right into it.

ariadne

I PUSH my eye open and my mind is punched with a hard fist of terror mixed with pain, and something akin to madness. A swirl of out-of-control emotions trying to thrust themselves deep inside my mind. Invasive, powerful, and all-consuming. I'm under attack from another Skilled—but like no Skilled I've ever felt before. The emotions are too raw, too unhinged, and reckless. I bring up my wall just in time, the barricade I use to isolate myself from other empaths. It's a struggle. Like trying to dam an angry, storm-ridden sea. Somehow, I manage to push it back, to hold my ground. I slowly drive those feelings out of my mind until there's nothing left behind except a single word…

Ariadne.

I take a few calming breaths. I'm shocked but okay. I can still feel *Ariadne* pushing at me, but now those emotions are muffled and distant and I can see them for what they are. This was no attack, but a dreadful scream of empathic madness.

What the hell did the Company do here?

There is only one conclusion that makes any sense. *Ariadne*, the bioship's brain, is an empathic entity like me. *A Skilled*, or some distorted version of one, but broadcasting on a more massive scale.

I need to find out more about *Ariadne*, about what happened here. To do that, I'd have to let the ship back inside my head and that ain't gonna happen again soon. Not if I want to preserve my sanity. Besides, keeping her at bay is sapping at my strength. Like trying to hold up a block of crushing granite.

Stranng gave me to midnight to solve this thing. I'm not sure I can resist *Ariadne's* powerful mind for that long. I now get why the Company wanted me aboard…

Using a Skilled to catch a Skilled.

Taking a few soothing breaths, I reassess the situation. I've still got a job to do and the quicker I do it the better. *Ariadne* or no. I force my mind to concentrate on where I am and what I'm doing. On the smashed pod's readouts—which are all flashing red.

I do a quick damage assessment of my own systems. No broken bones or internal injuries, although I have a lot of non-essential tissue damage. My helmet readout tells me my oxygen is in the amber. I don't have that long before my air is gonna run out. I need to get inside the ship asap.

Still… *I damn well made it.*

I imagine Stranng's consternation. He can't know I survived but even his compromised readouts would tell him I got inside the docking bay. That's one in the eye for him. The bigger danger was from *Ariadne* herself. I doubt he knew what he was sending me into.

I jettison the pod hatch, helped by a few kicks, and drop heavily on to the floor. I'm still full of adrenaline and, behind its haze, I can feel a growing ache. No matter how much the pod protected me, high-gee impacts are not to be sneezed at. It's gonna hurt and hurt bad. I tune down my pain but not enough to numb myself. Hurt is a motivating force and besides, it's my early warning system.

I stand on shaky legs. I'm still emaciated after my time spent in hypersleep before Stranng 'rescued me'. I'm functional... just. I'm met by a scene of devastation. Two battered and smashed transports lie in pieces. Bits of their internal components scattered about the docking area like the aftermath of a tornado. One side of the bay is scored by the impact of my arrival. Where the pod slammed into it, I guess—now a crushed, battered mess. I'll say one thing for the Company, their escape pods are better designed than their ships. They're usually only accessible to those with suitable rank. Self-preservation is very important to the Company, for those certain, important few that is. Hence the advanced dampening field stopping me from being pulped by all those gees of impact.

The possibility of a ship crashing into the cargo bay is not one the Company or any organisation ignores. The inner airlock is accessible via a sturdy, blast and crash-proof bulkhead. This ain't no basic shield—it's covered with something I've never seen on a Company ship, a beautiful etching of a vast spider sitting within an intricate web. The ship I glimpsed from hyperspace.

Ariadne.

A goddess from Greek myth. She oversaw the sacrificial labyrinth wherein lurked the Minotaur. I'm no Theseus, that's for sure. If I have to slay a beast with the body of a man and the head of a bull, I'm sure gonna be pissed. In comparison to what the Company has done here on this bioship, the myth of the minotaur is small beans.

If there's any monster aboard this ship, it's *Ariadne* herself.

I shake my head and enter the airlock. The heavy outer-hatch slides shut behind me. I punch the recycle. Nothing happens.

Huh?

I punch it again and still no reaction. There's no way the pod caused damage this far inside the ship. The airlock must've been shut down, deactivated intentionally. Alarm bells sound in my mind. With what happened with *Ariadne's* disturbed mind, I forgot what I was getting myself into. If I can't get inside the ship, I've no chance of solving what's beyond the airlock door and no chance at surviving longer than the air left in my suit.

I walk to the internal airlock door and peer out of the window, a small rounded portal. A young, petite female in fatigues—a Company ensign—lies on her back in the corridor beyond, like she fell where she was standing. I can't tell if she is alive or dead... but I don't hold out much hope. Her face is blotched, a bloated, purple tongue sticking out of her mouth like she's been strangled. If she hasn't perished, she soon will. My intuition tells me the girl was gassed by something nasty.

"What the fuck have you done here, *Ariadne?*" I whisper to myself.

Suddenly, getting out of the airlock and into the ship, doesn't seem like such a good idea any more. My skinsuit will protect me from any surface contaminants, but my air won't last forever. At some point, I'll have to breathe the ship's atmosphere.

The flash of shadows and two figures come hurrying into the outer airlock area, young kids barely out of their teens, wearing what look like low-ranking, ceremonial fleet personnel uniforms of white and orange although they're unfastened, sweaty and smudged. They carry rifles nestled into their shoulders, eyeing down the barrels and see me at once, the guns swivelling in my direction. I've nowhere to hide and do the only thing I can do. I shrug and raise my hands. I guess crashing my escape pod into the docking bay didn't go unnoticed.

One of the kids, short, sweaty looking with greased, slicked-back, black hair and equally greasy features, edges towards the airlock door and presses the com. "Who the hell are you? And how did you get aboard?" he blurts, an intense expression creasing his youthful face.

By the sublieutenant insignia on his cuffs, I guess he's the leader of this twosome. He's so short and stocky that his rifle is as big as he is.

The other kid stands tall and gangly at his side, sweat dripping down his face. He's a good-looking, short-haired blonde with striking, almost noble features. Intense blue eyes stare out of a face full of sadness and woe. Whatever has gone down on this ship has badly affected him. He wears the insignia of ensign, the fleet entry rank.

I realise they are just teenagers. They seem younger somehow. Maybe it's the fear etched into their faces. One thing is for sure, they don't look like hijackers. I drop my arms and patch my helmet into the airlock com. "You guys gonna let me aboard or what?"

The diminutive sublieutenant stabs his rifle in my direction. "I said, who are you? Answer the damn question!" His voice is no match for his words. Squeaky and stress-filled. He looks past me to see if I'm on my own.

"Who do you think I am?" I reply bullishly. "The Company ain't gonna let this ship fly away without sending in one of their top operatives. That happens to be me."

The kid looks confused. I try and make things a little easier for him. "Open the door! That's a direct order from your superior. Go inform the Strategist that I'm aboard. I want to talk to someone in charge, asap!"

The sublieutenant pulls back for a one-to-one with his blonde friend. While they chat, I take a guess that whatever went down on this ship hasn't helped their mood. Judging by their shaking heads, I'm betting they're less than keen about my arrival.

I want to try and read them, but that would let *Ariadne* back into my mind. And that's not ever going to happen. I can feel her madness crawling at the edge of my sensibilities, her tentacles writhing and probing. That would be suicide. I've become just as blind, just as ordinary as the next sucker—almost.

Another individual arrives in the airlock area. A tall, burly man in his forties, his skin light brown and greasy, with greying, curly hair that spills onto his vast shoulders. He wears the stained overalls of an engineer. He pulls up short when he sees me. I can tell by his shocked reaction that, even with my eye-patch and my one visible eye, he knows what I am.

"Who are you?" I ask over the com. He ignores me and strides over to the sublieutenant and joins in the discussion. His arrival results in more shaking heads and the flinging of arms. Disagreement. This carries on for some time until the big guy with the grey curly hair spins around and lumbers purposely towards the airlock. The Company grunts don't like this one bit. "Stand down, Hewlis!" the sublieutenant shouts, raising his gun.

Hewlis doesn't listen.

"I'll shoot!" the sublieutenant yells like a petulant child. "You know I will!"

The engineer raises his hands and stops, his lived-in eyes staring at me in apology. "The Company sent him here!" he rasps. "Can't you see that?"

"So, not everyone aboard this ship is an idiot," I say over the com.

"Shut your mouth!" the sublieutenant shouts at me.

"You gotta let him out, Drex," Hewlis pleads. "We need all the help we can get."

A low beep from my skinsuit helmet and the amber air readout flashes red. "If you don't let me out of here soon, I'm gonna run out of oxy—"

The greasy-haired kid, Drex, offs the com. What happens next is another intense argument, but Drex and his friend outnumber Hewlis two to zero. Two guns that is. Which will win most arguments. As for me, the result ain't that good. Hewlis doesn't want to give up without a fight, but it's as I said—guns always win out—especially if a pair of grunts wield them.

I don't get it? I hit the ship with quite a clunk. Why would the strategist send down a couple of green-ass low rankers and an engineer to go check it out? The answer ain't a palatable one. *The Strategist is dead or injured.*

Drex and the blonde kid escort a scowling Hewlis away.

The red flashing in my helmet becomes insistent.

Damn! The last thing I expected was to get stopped at the first hurdle. I'm hoping Drex and the rest have gone to find someone with more authority to sort this out. I have no choice but to wait. With my air running low, that ain't gonna be easy. But I ain't one of the Skilled for nothing.

I sit down, propping myself against the airlock wall, slowing my heart and respiration, closing everything down other than my vital systems. I can survive in a self-induced coma for an hour or two without oxygen. Not that this ship has that long. Hopefully, whoever's in charge will come get me before that time runs out.

I concentrate on my heartbeat—now a distant thud. Filling the time between each extended beat with small bursts of brain electricity. I leave the airlock behind and enter a deep meditative state…

vatic

SOMEONE IS slapping my face. I open my eyes to see Hewlis standing over me, his brown eyes flashing with concern. My heart lurches back into scudding action and quickly I throw up my wall. This time I'm ready for *Ariadne's* invasive and insane mind. It's still a struggle, but I push her quickly away. I take a deep breath of warm ship air. Despite any worries about gas or poison, I'm instantly re-energised. If there's something nasty in the ship's atmosphere, I can't smell it.

"Thanks," I say, pushing myself angrily to my feet, legs creaking with the effort.

"Don't thank me," Hewlis replies, towering over me like a bear. "I didn't open the airlock. You look terrible."

"I'll survive," I bark back at him, breathing heavily. "I'm Vatic. And that's what I'm famous for… surviving."

"Vatic." He repeats the word mechanically.

"Yeah, just Vatic. Don't overuse it."

Sublieutenant Drex pushes the tired-looking engineer aside. "How come you're still alive?" he asks, sounding disappointed. "Your suit was in the red."

"Like I said, I don't kill that easy. I guess it was you who let me out? Cos that was a good decision."

Drex shrugs, a confused expression on his youthful face. "Not me," he says, his voice an exaggerated squeak. "The airlock opened by itself. We thought you were dead."

I glance over to the sad-looking blonde kid. "What's your name?"

He points his rifle at me. "Ensign Murton Boyd." His voice is full of emotion. The kid is choked.

What the hell has gone down here?

I turn my attention back to Drex. "Just how fucking old are you both?"

"You can't talk to us like that!" he bleats.

"I'll talk to a little piss-ant like you any way I want. I haven't forgotten that it was you who left me in the airlock to suffocate to death."

Drex stares into my one, wired, manic-looking eye and I see that same flicker of recognition I've had all my life. "You… *you really are a Skilled,*" he says.

My eyes, like all others of my breed, have a certain *look*. Like we're on drugs. Manic almost. And even though the range of colours match those of regular humans, our eyes have an intensity that is difficult to ignore. Mine are a bright, wired, and startling blue. Although, I've only got one on show.

"Of course he's a Skilled!" Hewlis replies with exasperation. "I told you what he was. Not that you believed me. Who else could get aboard a ship during hyperspace and still be alive after his suit's oxygen ran out? They're a breed apart." He flashes his brown eyes in my direction. "No offence."

I shrug. "You'd have to try a lot harder to offend me." The issue with the airlock and who decided to let me out, can wait for now. I have far more important concerns. "Listen up," I say. "The *Ariadne* is heading towards rival Company space which means that if we don't stop her and stop her soon, we're all gonna go boom-boom." I'm using Stranng's words—I want to be sure the message gets across without any confusion.

The news hits Drex and his young friend hard. Hewlis grits his teeth, his grizzled lower jaw rising to form a grimace. Hopefully the information will focus their minds. I need everyone working together if we're gonna get out of this mess.

"What do you mean, go boom-boom?" Drex asks.

"Where do you think I came from? A puff of damn smoke? A Company ship is shadowing the *Ariadne* out there in hyperspace. I happen to know the Strategist in charge. He's got one hell of a twitchy trigger finger, you get me, Sublieutenant?"

Drex doesn't like being talked to like this, that much is obvious.

I pull myself up to my full-diminutive height and take a deep breath. "I need to know what's been going on here. You can start by telling me why there's a dead body outside the airlock."

"You're not giving the orders around here," Drex says, bristling as if this is a playground power play. "You're under arrest until I say otherwise. Skilled or not."

"And what gives you the authority to put me in chains?" I ask, aware of a cloying heat. Company ships are normally a lot cooler. No wonder Boyd and Drex are sweating like pigs.

"Our Strategist and all other senior officers are dead," Hewlis explains calmly. "Sublieutenant Drex here, is the only surviving fleet officer of rank." He raises his eyebrows at me in a way that says the kid ain't up to the job, but I can see that for myself.

"Dead?" I take in the information with an annoyed shake of my head. I'll find out exactly how they died later. First, I need to stamp my authority. "I'm taking command as of now," I say to Drex. "You get me?"

A relieved smile passes over Hewlis' ruddy face.

Drex shakes his head. "No way. You don't look like no Company Grandee to me. Where's your uniform? Where's your ID?"

I point to my one remaining eye. "This is all the ID I fucking need."

Drex ain't impressed. "You don't have the rank, you don't have—"

I slap the kid in the face.

Drex is shocked, his eyebrows furrowing, fingers tightening on his rifle.

I slap him a second time and a third, jabbing a quick elbow into his guts, and, with a twist of my other hand, his rifle is in my possession.

Boyd shouts, his gun now pointing at my head but he's uncertain.

"Like I said, I'm taking command." I slam the rifle back in to Drex's hands. "Attention, Sublieutenant!" I bark.

Drex stands there, motionless, a look of suppressed anger twisting at his face.

"Listen up! My name is Vatic, I'm a full member of the Secondary Executive, giving me authority over you, your warrant officer, your strategist, and the goddamn rear admiral of the Company fleet if it comes to that. Which means that when I say jump, you jump, you get me?"

Drex makes the wise decision and draws himself to reluctant attention—but I haven't broken him yet. In response, Boyd drops the rifle to his side and dutifully salutes. Like I've always said, grunts prefer someone with real authority in charge.

I push through them, exit the airlock, and go over to the body on the floor—the girl I spotted earlier. A blackened tongue sticks out of her mouth, like a frozen scream, her eyes wide open and staring with a look of terror—a clear sign of asphyxiation. Like I thought, she's dead. But even though her body lies outside the airlock, she hasn't died from depressurisation. There are no tell tell-tale skin blemishes—just blotchy patches. *A toxin of some kind.*

"How many other survivors?"

"Seven," Hewlis answers.

"Seven?" I turn towards him. "Out of forty-three?"

The engineer shrugs, his mammoth shoulders rising and falling in a practised gesture. "I guess so."

"You said the Strategist and the other officers are dead. Did they all die like this?"

Drex draws breath to speak but I'm still pissed at him for leaving me to die in the airlock. "Not you," I say. I turn my attention to Boyd, who seems a lot more relaxed about me being in charge. "What happened, kid?"

"It started a little over two hours ago," Boyd answers, tears forming in the corners of his eyes, his voice thick with emotion. "Twenty-hundred hours ship time. The air supply was poisoned. Some kind of gas, I guess, sir,"

"You sure that's what it was?"

Boyd nods, a distraught look crossing his face. "We were heading towards the Hospitality Suite on ceremonial duties for tonight's VIP party. You know the type of thing? Stand by the doors looking smart when…"

"When what, Ensign?" I bark.

Drex and Boyd swap glances.

"Out with it!"

"We were in the ship's elevator, sir," Boyd says. "It's off-limits, but… but we were late and thought it would be quicker than the stairs. We walked inside, the doors closed and… the thing got stuck between floors. When the elevator finally started moving again, we emerged to find everybody dead and a strange smell in the air."

The tears that were forming in Boyd's eyes, now drip down his cheek in twin streams. He wipes them away with the back of his hand.

"You okay, recruit?"

He nods. Whatever happened aboard the *Ariadne* has hit him hard. Maybe too hard. "The other survivors, where are they?"

"In Hospitality," Hewlis replies, the engineer's large brown eyes red with tiredness. "That's where we left them when Drex ordered me to try and break into the bridge with him and Boyd."

I take in the information with a nod of my head. Something doesn't feel right here. I remember the wafer stuffed inside my skinsuit and pull it free, tapping the screen into life. It's just as Stranng said, a roster of names and ranks—forty-three of them, and not more than a paragraph or two about each. Is this all I've been given to work with? ...Shit!

I glance at the time:

21:52

Two hours to midnight, give or take. To solve this thing. I wonder if I can last that long under the terrible assault of *Ariadne's* mind.

I access the roster again. The wafer tells me nothing extra about Drex or Boyd other than they're fleet low-rankers just starting out. Drex's promotion to sublieutenant was nothing special—regular career progression for a keen recruit. And Drex is the keen type, that's for sure.

I breathe deeply. The ship air is warmer than normal and smells stale with a hint of antiseptic— missing the all-pervading stink of sweat and piss. "What happened to the toxin?"

Boyd shrugs, pulling himself together. "Whatever was in the air dissipated, I guess."

"If everyone is dead, who's flying the ship?"

"No one is flying the *Ariadne!*" Drex blurts, unable to keep quiet. "The bridge is in lockdown and the security cams show everyone dead inside. That's why we've been trying to break in. We need to get back control as soon as possible, especially now that we know we're heading towards rival space."

"No one is flying her? Why would someone poison the crew and everybody else if not to gain control of the goddamn ship? And even if they somehow got access to *Ariadne's* nav-systems, why fly her to the Company's closest rival? No enemy agent would be so stupid as to head for home. That'd be suicide, not without backup from other ships. They'd instead try and hide *Ariadne* somewhere out of the way."

"She must be flying on autopilot," Hewlis says and, even without my empathy, I can tell he believes there's more to it than that.

"We need to get back control of *Ariadne*," Drex says, before I can answer the engineer. "If there's another Company ship out there waiting to blow us up, that has to be our priority."

I take a deep breath. "Be quiet Sublieutenant. What you think is now unimportant. I've taken charge of this shit-show. We're doing nothing until I get a clear chain of events. I want to know what happened here. Step by step."

Drex looks like he might explode. I realise a few slaps ain't gonna be enough to get him in line. I turn to Hewlis. "You. Take me through what happened."

Hewlis nods, his lived-in eyes closing for a second. "The ship has been preparing for this evening's VIP function for a couple of days now," he begins. "Some swanky gathering to show off the *Ariadne*. We were in standard orbit around a Company planet. Awaiting arrivals."

"Who organised the party?" I ask.

"Professor Anil Chandrasekhar," The burly

engineer replies with a curl of his lip. "He's the egghead behind the design of the whole ship. The *Ariadne* is his project, his design…"

velez

"CHANDRASEKHAR?" THE name is unfamiliar.

I check the roster.

> *Professor Anil Chandrasekhar.*
> *Age: 162.*
> *Cereb specialist.*

Cereb. Short for 'cerebellum'—*brain matter.* And the *Ariadne* is a bioship. I can understand why the Company wants to use a human brain to run a warship, or more precisely, a Skilled brain. That at least makes sense. Even if what they have done here sickens me.

Computers developed exponentially in the early days of their construction, but the curve soon slowed and levelled. The result? Stalemate. When all your rivals have identical battle computers, no one has the upper-hand.

It was this stalemate that led to the companies investing in banned genetic manipulation. An illegal attempt to boost the human part of the equation.

That's where I came into the story. Me and the other Skilled.

When Earth learned of what the companies were doing, that they were flouting 'Earth Law', their programs were shut down and the Skilled taken away to live out their lives in Internment. That soon changed after the Companies revolted. Earth lost its power to a conglomeration of vested interest. To turnover and greed. To a percentage calculation of profit over loss.

I can't be too bitter. It was that change that led to my freedom. And I admit it, in those early days, I loved the Company. I lived for it.

Until the inevitable war.

Without the balance of an independent Earth, the Companies ended up fighting over a fucking resource map, where the resources were suns, planets, moons, and entire solar systems.

The Company—*my Company*—was the victor… or at least it came out on top. Annexing Earth. Relocating its First Executive Board onto the home planet. But not without cost… The war was destructive. It's taken quite a few years for the Company to rebuild, to get back to where it once was. The other companies have also been busy. Borders have been strengthened and many warships patrol them. That's why *Ariadne* has come into being. This bioship must be an attempt to gain the upper hand, to end the stalemate forever. But whatever Chandrasekhar was trying to create here has gone gravely wrong.

"Chandrasekhar?" I say finally. "Is he one of the survivors?"

"He was the guest of honour," Boyd answers, wiping beads of sweat from his forehead. "He was expected to give a speech to the party of VIPs." Boyd's bottom lip trembles. "The last time I saw him was this morning. Arguing with the ship's Strategist again. The professor is now probably dead with everyone else."

I ignore Boyd's conjecture. "Arguing?"

He nods. "An ongoing thing. Those two have been at loggerheads for months now."

"Over what?"

"It's not my place to say."

"Just tell me!"

"Small things mostly. They didn't get on."

"And tonight's party? The *Ariadne* was in a stationary orbit—waiting for the guests to arrive, is that it?"

"I assume so," Hewlis answers. "But I'm an engineer not a maître d'."

"That's right, sir," Boyd continues. "The guests all arrived on board this evening. Ferried in by our transports."

My mind goes back to the smashed cargo bay and the destroyed ships, but I don't let myself get distracted. "Then what?"

"They were escorted to Hospitality. Just a straightforward Company gathering," Boyd continues as if he'd been to a few himself, although his expression tells me this was nothing like anything he'd seen before. "Guests, consorts, officers and a few waiters. Me and Drex were to be stationed by the door. Everything was normal until…" his voice dries, his eyes flicking over to the dead ensign lying on the floor just a few feet away. "Until everyone died."

"And you heard nothing about a murder?"

"A murder?" Hewlis says, his eyebrows rising to disappear behind his thick, curly greying hair.

"Let me explain," I say, fixing the burly engineer with my one good eye. "Before the ship jumped into hyperspace, which I guess was before everyone was gassed, the coms-officer sent out a mayday. It said they'd been locked out of the ship, and that there had been a murder aboard. I don't know who the victim was... not yet, anyway, but I'm sure the two events are linked in some way. If I find who was killed and why, maybe I can make sense of this whole thing. So, let me ask you all again... did you witness anything out-of-the-ordinary before the gas attack?"

A shake of heads.

I stare back at the two low-rankers. "Have you searched the ship?"

Drex swaps a glance with Boyd. "What's the point?" he says with exasperation.

Before I can reply, a woman arrives in chef's fatigues, a thin, dark-skinned Hispanic whose expression shows intrigue at my appearance, slowing her steps as she notices me, before striding purposely over.

"What're you doing here?" Drex shouts, rounding on her. "I ordered everyone to stay put in the Hospitality Suite while we were attempting to get access to the bridge."

The chef eyes Drex with disdain. I can see from her expression that she's as impressed with the kid as

I am. "Who are you?" she asks me with more authority than her displayed rank of Third Chef would suggest.

"I'm the schmuck the Company has put in charge to get to the bottom of this goddamn mess. What's of more importance is… *who are you?*"

The woman glances at Hewlis for confirmation.

He nods, widening his eyes.

"I'm Chef Velez," she replies, like the name should mean something to me.

"From the catering corps?"

"Yeah. Although I'm a lot more than a simple caterer." Her voice is all calm, yet I can see the fast beat of her heart in the twitch of her neck.

The woman possesses a peculiar beauty. Her eyes are slightly misaligned, her nose hooked and a little crooked, yet it works for her. She doesn't look or sound like a Third Chef Technician to me. Velez carries herself with the authority that comes from long experience of ordering people around. She's in her forties, making this exotic specimen too old for such a lowly rank. Third Chef translates to 'chopping duty', the job of a teenager or someone starting out. She's an enigma. Without my empath skills to help me, she could be hiding any number of sins.

"At ease, Velez. The cavalry's just arrived. Or haven't you worked that out yet?" I say.

She takes a few calming breaths and the twitching stops.

I tap at my wafer.

Jurado Velez.
Age: 46.

Company Designate: Third Chef Technician.

Holder of some quite impressive culinary awards. I read on. She was demoted from the top galley rank of Executive Chef, but there's no reason why.

"It says here you're a whizz with food? What the hell did you do to get busted?"

Velez's green eyes stare at me, unfazed by the question, and I glimpse a fire within her.

"I upset the wrong person," she replies enigmatically. "I'm one of the best chefs in the Company and they did this to me." She points a knife-scarred finger at her uniform and sneers.

I carry on reading the wafer. There's a date for when she joined the *Ariadne* but since Stranng woke me out of hypersleep on that colony ship, god knows how many days ago, I'm out of my reckoning. "How long have you been aboard?"

"Two days. I requested the assignment. The more VIP functions I can cater for, the better my chances of getting my rank back," she says, although I'm not sure I believe her.

"How did you survive?"

"I was in the galley," Velez answers. "In the cold-storage area on my own with the door closed."

"What were you doing in there?"

"Despite my lowly rank," Velez spits, "I was still expected to work on my famous signature desserts. I am an artist who demands perfection, which means absolutely no interference. That's why I was inside and alone. When I emerged…" A frown crosses her features. "I found everyone dead."

I'm wasting time—I guess they all have a similar story—and decide to move things along.

"Okay," I say, addressing them all. "This is how things are gonna go down. First, I want to visit the bridge and take a look at that com feed for myself. Then I'm gonna head to Hospitality and interrogate the rest of the survivors. In the meantime, I require a head-count of everyone aboard the *Ariadne*. Dead or alive. And if they're dead, an assessment on how they died. The Company roster says forty-three souls aboard. If there's anybody else on this ship who shouldn't be, I need to know about it. If you find more survivors, take them to the Hospitality Suite. I'm gonna make that my temporary HQ." I turn to Drex and Boyd. "I want you two to take care of that."

"A head-count!" Drex fumes. "When we're racing towards enemy space? Are you mad? We should be trying to break into the bridge or disabling the Snag Drive. I don't care about who you are or where you're from, you ain't telling me what to do."

Apart from the rifle, Drex carries a buzz-gun on his waist. I step up to him, my face next to his. "Give me your side-arm, Sublieutenant!" He pauses in indecision, which is all the motivation I need.

I snap the gun from its holster. And, in one quick motion, pistol-whip him to the floor. "I'm not gonna ask you to do things twice… you get me?"

Drex is stunned, not from the actual blow—I didn't hit him that hard. I don't think he's ever been treated like this, which must come as a shock to the kid. It's the second time I've beat up on him and, I admit, I'm enjoying myself. I point the gun at his head.

"Don't you think I want to get off this damn ship just as much as everyone else?" I say. "With the bridge in lock-down, it'd take you days to breakthrough. Days we don't have. It's a waste of our time. The fact remains… *Ariadne* is heading for one big explosion in hyperspace in under two hours if we don't stop her. The way I look at it, you either help me by doing what you're told, when you're told or… you're just as useless as this corpse and the others on this goddamn ghost ship. Believe me, at this point, I'm quite happy to let you join them."

My little performance is just that, a performance. If I'm gonna get these idiots out of this mess, I need to play hard and I need to play rough. There's no time for anything less. Would I shoot the kid? Maybe? Who knows? But self-preservation sure is one motivating force.

Drex nods.

"Say it!"

"Yes, sir."

"Good."

Boyd pulls Drex to his feet, a look of determination upon his grief-ridden features.

I take Drex's belt and holster the buzz-gun to my waist. "Get that roster back to me asap. Dismissed!"

Drex wipes his nose and he, and Boyd, quickly disappear into the corridors.

"That was a little rough," Hewlis says.

"You wanna make a complaint? Then I suggest you do it to the Company, when you get the chance that is. From this point on, you'll do what I say when I say it. You get me?"

Hewlis nods but Velez stands her ground. "What did you mean… *we're heading for an explosion?*"

I tell her about *Ariadne's* destination, and Stranng shadowing us in hyperspace.

Velez ain't impressed to say the least. "I don't like Drex or his friend," she says, the twitch returning to her neck, "but he does have a point. What will questioning the survivors achieve? If the priority is to get this ship out of hyperspace, aren't you wasting time?"

"The kid needed slapping down, don't make me do the same to you," I bark, wondering why it's so hard for this goddamn crew to follow orders.

"I just don't want to die," Velez continues. "Like everyone else."

"You want that kid back in charge?"

Velez shakes her head.

"Good. Cos I'm the only chance you've got."

cereb

VELEZ, HEWLIS and me make our way out of the airlock area and head for the bridge, passing occasional portholes revealing the beautiful swirl of hyperspace beyond. I see the vast, glowing arms again, stretching out from the ship like the crooked legs of a spider. *Ariadne's* Snag Drive array—an unusual design for a warship or any Company ship—and no doubt the reason for this ship's legendary arachnid name. The Snag Drive is usually a more stunted and less efficient affair, squatting underneath a ship like an upturned crown, making it less vulnerable to attack. *Ariadne's* array would make her a sitting duck. The thought reminds me that Strategist Stranng is out there somewhere. Knowing that his finger is itching on the damn trigger ain't comforting, that's for sure. With me gone, he's off the hook. Especially after what I threatened him with when I came back from that mess I found in the Zeta-Karst Laboratories. He has one redeeming quality—the man is a fully-fledged Company bastard. He's not the type to disobey an order. He ain't got the imagination.

The *Ariadne* is a compact ship. The outer corridor follows the hull with a visible curve. I'm impressed. Flowing lines are not normal in Company designs. They prefer hard edges and right-angles. This ship has been built to an aesthetic I've not previously seen before. There is attention to detail even in the corridor I'm now walking down. The floor appears to be sprung and is covered in a burgundy coloured carpet. Gone is the clatter and thump of footsteps, instead walking is more like gliding. The walls are still cream in colour but banded with gold and silver with not a bolt or rivet in sight. The lighting is less harsh and comes from the walls themselves rather than from fixed, bright points.

Ariadne has been designed to calm the senses, rather than to jar them.

If I didn't know this was a Company ship, I'd have guessed it was a cruise-liner for those too old and too rich to do anything else with their time and money, other than to swan around the galaxy in the height of luxury until they drew their last pampered breath.

I turn to Hewlis, waving my wafer in his direction. "Flash me over the ship's schematics."

Hewlis complies, his own wafer making an appearance. A few taps later I receive the file and bring it up in 3D. The *Ariadne* sure has an interesting look. I flip the image around with my finger. The fuselage is rounded like a giant extended egg sack. The matter engine and hyperspace array looking even more spider-like than from the portholes. I shrug at Hewlis. *"Ariadne,* huh?"

"I never did like spiders," he says.

I can understand his dislike. Arachnids, and a whole horde of other bugs, found their way onto ships hundreds of years ago, along with humanity's other ever-present companions, *rats*. Add all that cosmic radiation in those unprotected areas of the ship where vermin hang out and spaceships developed their own mini-ecosystems. The Company doesn't care about them. Evolution is a harsh mistress. These creatures have learned to live in a mostly peaceful symbiosis with the ships they inhabit. Infestations have occasionally gotten out of control, but I doubt a new ship like the *Ariadne* would have such problems.

I bring up a more detailed view. The superstructure consists of a series of well-defined decks with the bridge, officer decks and habitation at the top and engineering levels at the bottom. The central decks house the matter engine and various other ship systems. A main elevator, an unnecessary luxury as far as I can tell, is located at the ship's centre, surrounded by a staircase with various other stairs dotted here and there. The Hospitality Suite is located under the bridge, facing forwards, next to the canteen and galley. For such a small ship, this suite is over-sized. Most of the Company vessels don't have a dedicated area for Hospitality at all. Any dignitaries would usually be hosted in the Officer's Mess. A cramped room at best.

The ship sure is ostentatious. What Professor Chandrasekhar has created here is impressive. But it is nothing more than the painted facade of a mausoleum. Finery built to distract us from the evil squatting at the centre of its web, the insane spider,

Ariadne.

The Hospitality Suite and the survivors are on the same level as the cargo dock—the level I'm standing on—and I'm tempted to visit there first, but I need to look at the bridge for myself.

Do I doubt what Drex and Hewlis told me?

Without my empathy in place, my answer must be 'yes'. I need to make sure that the bridge is as inaccessible as they say it is. I doubt my name is still in the system, but if so, I also might be able to use my rank to undo the lockdown. A small hope but worth a try.

While we are walking, I flick through the ship's levels, trying to locate its computer-core. Then I remember, the ship is experimental. Run by organics, by *Ariadne*—not computers. I shudder at the thought, wiping at the sweat on my face. "Why is it so damn hot in here?" I ask.

"There's something wrong with the cooling system," Hewlis explains, his exaggerated shrug making a reappearance. "I'm not sure what's happened."

We come across occasional bodies also looking like they died where they fell. Whatever killed them was quick, that's for sure. I examine them and discover nothing new. They all died the same way. Velez and Hewlis find my interest in the dead unpalatable. Bodies have never bothered me. It's the alive who cause all the problems...*mostly.* I've been responsible for far more than forty-three corpses in my time. Millions more. I don't have time for guilty reminiscence.

A stab from my stomach. "I'm hungry," I announce,

turning over yet another body, its blackened face leering up at me. "Is there anything to eat and drink on this goddamn ship?"

Velez pulls a disgusted face. "What do you think the crew eats? Air?" she replies.

I ignore her attitude and smile. "Good. Cos I'm starving." I drop the body back down. "I'll also need some cigarettes. You smoke?" Both Hewlis and Velez shake their heads. Typical. No one smokes no more. I stand up. "About these survivors. You say there's seven, yeah?"

"Eight, if we now count you," says Hewlis. "That was quite some feat—getting aboard."

"I'm not asking for damn compliments," I snap back at him. "It's a straightforward process. I ask a question, you answer. Get me?"

The engineer's mouth twists into a smile. "Yeah. I get you," he replies. "There's seven survivors, not counting the ones Drex and Boyd might find. I don't hold out much hope that they'll be able to add anyone."

"And why do you think that?"

"The guests were all in the Hospitality Suite, most of whom are dead. Any surviving crew members would know to make their way to the bridge. No one turned up when we were there, trying to break in."

"About that… didn't you tell Drex that the bridge is designed to keep the Strategist and the crew safe in case of an incursion? It'd take days to get through a bridge door in lock-down mode."

Hewlis shrugs again, another long, drawn out affair. "You've met Drex. He didn't want to listen…

and what else could we do? You might not want to hear this, but the kid has a point. If we can't get onto the bridge, there's no way we can regain control of the ship."

I point at his stained overalls. "I thought you were an engineer? Don't you have an innate knowledge of the *Ariadne?*"

His wet brown eyes narrow in the bulbous skin of his face. "I'm just a regular grunt brought in to look after the regular systems," he says. "I wasn't part of the advanced bio-team—the new systems, which pervade the ship like a spider's web, were off-limits to me. I don't have the right pay grade. I should never have come here. The ship isn't right. I had a bad feeling about her from the off. And if you're an engineer, you learn to trust your gut."

Engineers are well known for their superstitious beliefs—which is odd for such a qualified profession. He may be sensing *Ariadne's* madness as 'uneasiness'. I can feel the full force of her insanity as a constant wave upon the empathic spectrum, a wave I'm struggling to keep at bay. The look on the engineer's face tells me he has more to say.

"Spit it out," I say to him.

Hewlis chews his cheeks for a few seconds, anger sparkling in his eyes. "What the Company has done here is evil," he rasps. "They wrap the thing up in pretty words. *Bio-intelligence. Cereb. The brain.* But this is human experimentation and nothing else. It's been outlawed as long as I know. The damn thing is inhumane!"

My empathy may be off-line, but I can tell he means

what he says. I agree with him. It's no regular human brain squatting at the centre of this bioship, but one of my breed, a breed apart from humans. The Cereb is a genetically engineered control system using the same empathic abilities as myself and others like me.

"Were you naïve enough to think this kind of thing wasn't going on?" I ask. "That the Company cares anything about sanctions or laws?"

Hewlis sags, the anger leaving him. He takes a deep calming breath, his head shaking from side to side. "Of course not. I just never expected to become part of it—*to get this close*. I'm an engineer. I work with coolant systems and boosters. With hydraulic pressures and fuel quotients. What they're doing here doesn't require engineers but goddamn surgeons and psych-teks. I wanted nothing more to do with the project once I learned what was going on. I tried to get reassigned, tried to do anything to get myself transferred off this damn ghost ship… You know the Company. What I wanted meant squat."

Listening to the engineer's words, I can't help but agree with his sentiment.

I swipe the wafer and bring up the man's details.

Hewlis Gray.
Age: 45.
Fourth Engineer.

Fourth engineer is a low rank for someone of his age in this profession. He has served on an extensive list of ships, too many of them. He's been moved on more times than has been healthy for his career.

Maybe he's a troublemaker, one of those people who rubs everyone else up the wrong way? He's a big guy, naturally large. I sure wouldn't want to be on the wrong side of him. So far, all I've gotten from the man is good vibes, apart from his obvious disdain at what's been going on aboard the *Ariadne*. Yet there is something about him I can't quite put my finger on. "You didn't tell me how you survived?"

Hewlis rubs at his face, his hand, rasping against half a day's growth of greyed, patchy stubble. "I was in the hold, working in a depressurised service area. Just routine stuff. When I got back into the ship, everyone was dead and that jumped up squirt, Drex, had put himself in charge."

"Another convenient story," I say. Hewlis doesn't react. He's either very much in control of himself or he doesn't care.

We continue along the ship's central corridor until we reach the elevator and stairwell. The elevator doors are decorated in a cool art-deco design. Stylised and like nothing I've ever seen before.

The air here is even more cloying, accompanied by the aroma of... "Is that burning?" I ask.

Velez sniffs the air, a worried look on her face, her neck starting to twitch again. "Smells like cooked meat."

We follow the growing stench, entering a side corridor until we arrive at a service panel. "It seems to be coming from here," I say to Hewlis.

We look at each other.

"Open it," I say. "It's your goddamn ship, even if you hate it."

Hewlis pulls at the hatch. "Hot," he says, producing an oily rag from his pocket and wrapping it around his hand. "That ain't right." He pulls again at the hatch, straining. "It's jammed."

For a big man, he seems peculiarly weak. "Put your damn back into it!"

Hewlis gives me a sideways look and braces against the wall. The hatch opens with a pop and we are hit by a cloud of sweet-smelling steam, heavy with the aroma of cooked flesh. I shutdown my olfactory system and diminish my breathing to nothing more than a rasp. Hewlis seems unaffected, although Velez starts to retch. The fog clears and Hewlis peers inside. "What the goddamn hell?"

flesh

I PUSH Hewlis aside and stare into the open hatch. A mixture of tubes, wires and… *burnt flesh*. A pipe glows red and what looks like charred, burnt meat has peeled away from it, accompanied by a network of shrivelled nerves and other organic tissue. "Part of the bio-systems?" I ask Hewlis, allowing myself to breathe normally again, expecting his trademark shrug.

"Shit," he says, flicking through his wafer. "I think this is why the ship is so goddamn hot. "It's the air-con system."

"Air-con?" I reply. "You mean the supply of oxygen? Sounds serious."

Hewlis ignores me for a few more moments while he flicks at his wafer. "No, these are environmental controls," he says finally. "The system that regulates temperature throughout the ship. It's responsible for air circulation, for diverting warm air from the engines and other systems to the colder outer hull areas and vice-versa."

"And it's failed?"

Hewlis pokes inside the hatch, a grimace across his face. "Yeah, the organic component has literally been fried."

"What caused this?"

"How the hell should I know?" Hewlis spits back at me. "Like I said, all this stuff is way past my pay-grade."

"But it's not serious? Not life-threatening?"

He shakes his head. "No, it just means that some parts of the ship will be either warmer or colder than is comfortable, which we've already discovered."

"Could other systems be affected?"

"Who knows? Unless there's a system-wide failure, that information won't be sent to my wafer. Instead, everything is monitored from the bridge. We'd need to get inside for a damage report and that ain't possible."

"There's no other data-centres or terminals?"

"The ship ain't a conventional design," Hewlis explains, sounding annoyed. "Normally there'd be hook-ups we could use to interrogate the computer. To get access and readouts. But not on the *Ariadne*."

I stare back into the open hatch—the flesh extends past the inspection panel and into the superstructure. "Could this be the system that was used to gas the crew and everybody else on board?"

Hewlis shuffles his feet beside me. "Yeah. But not anymore. Not with this damage."

I turn to face him. "Did someone wilfully sabotage *Ariadne* to prevent her gassing the ship again?"

Hewlis rubs at his grizzled chin, the loose flesh of his cheeks bulging. "Possibly. But who?"

"That's what I'm gonna find out. Someone is fighting back, which is the first good news I've heard since I've arrived on this goddamn ship. Let's get out of here."

We return to the elevator. "This is usually off-limits to the likes of you and me," Hewlis says with a smile. "What do you say we travel in style?"

"How many floors up to the bridge?" I ask.

Hewlis hits the call button. "Too many."

The elevator arrives with a hum and the doors open to reveal golden walls decorated with more art-deco fluting. "So, this is for bridge officers only, huh?"

"I think it was for Chandrasekhar's personal use," Hewlis says with disdain. "Although I've seen others use the elevator. And if you believe Drex and Boyd, they got stuck between floors in it."

"You think they were lying?" I ask.

"I don't know what to think," Hewlis replies. "You're the investigator... I'm just an engineer, remember?"

I'm weak, still emaciated from my extended time in hypersleep, but I'm not the type to take the easy route. It's not in my DNA... literally. "We'll use the stairs."

Hewlis points to the open elevator. "We can be there in seconds."

"Like I said, we'll use the damn stairs! I can't risk the thing malfunctioning for a second time, you get me? Is everyone on this ship as belligerent as each other?"

Hewlis grimaces. "You're in charge."

The spiral stairs twist around the outside of the

elevator, a dizzying drop over a simple handrail to the bottom deck many floors below. We start to climb, and I immediately regret my decision. My legs are wobbly and my heart pounds in my ears. I'm also starting to feel the effect of that bruising landing in the cargo bay. I check my system. Everything is in balance, I'm just undernourished and a little battered. I increase oxygen intake, tone down my pain receptors even further—any more and I'll be almost numb—and trudge on.

The air becomes dramatically cooler as we climb. I wipe my forehead, ridding it of cold sweat and shaking it away. We're closer to the hull, shown by the tightening of the ship's natural curves. The deep cold of hyperspace is leaking into the ship. I'm still suffering from the effects of my prolonged hypersleep—but then again cold, hard space is only a few feet away. In that regard, hyperspace is no different. There's still a vacuum. It's still hundreds of degrees below zero and it will still kill you if you go out there unprotected.

Next to me, Hewlis also seems to be struggling. His bulk is about twice that of mine. He has a lot more weight to shift. "Shouldn't you be used to moving around a spaceship this way?" I ask him.

All I get in reply is his habitual shrug.

We ascend the floors and finally emerge on the command deck. I'm out of breath and wheezing.

"You okay?" Velez ventures. She's not even winded.

"I'm fine," I reply. "It's been a long couple of days. Nothing that a shot of whisky wouldn't cure." I nod for Hewlis to lead us on.

More bodies lie in the central corridor up here.

I stop and examine each one of them, adding their details to my wafer. I'm in a rush to sort out this mess aboard the *Ariadne*, but a Skilled never leaves a stone unturned. Or a body. It's a ridiculous cliché, but true of my breed. The need to examine everything and everyone is a compulsion hardwired into us at the genetic level.

More jumbled corpses inhabit a darkened side corridor. I enter, crouching down to check them out.

"I'm not sure what you're hoping to find," says Velez coming up behind me.

"This," I say, turning over one of the bodies. A tall, imposing-looking woman wearing a long black jacket, white shirt and ruffles—dressed for tonight's party. Her stomach is an empty bloodied hole, the obvious result of a buzz-gun shot.

bridge

A QUICK search of the dead woman's clothing reveals a few personal items and her Company ID. Her rather pompous name is *Mandibald Glaxtinian*, one of the grandees invited to the party and an impressive one at that.

I take out my wafer and search for the woman.

> *Mandibald Glaxtinian.*
> *Age: 46.*
> *Projects Arbiter.*

Arbiter? The title is a Company euphemism for *ball-breaker*. Someone brought into a project with the sole intention of knocking a few heads together or shutting it down. Having her aboard would've made everyone nervous, especially Professor Chandrasekhar who oversaw the ship and its construction. There're a few details of Glaxtinian's Company history—all very impressive. She was on a steep Company career curve, until someone shot her in the gut that is, and, judging by the wound, quite badly at that. This woman was taken out by an amateur or that's what they wanted everyone to think.

The death of someone like this will cause quite a wave, but the Company is willing to kill everyone aboard the *Ariadne* to prevent her from reaching rival company space. When it comes to the Company, everyone is expendable.

I check the other bodies around her. They all died via asphyxiation and none of them are carrying weapons.

"Looks like you were right," says Hewlis. "Someone *was* murdered."

"Either of you know who she is?" I ask.

Hewlis shrugs whilst Velez says nothing.

"You deaf, Velez?" I bark, standing up on shaky legs.

Velez stares at the blooded corpse, a pleased look on her face. "She's just another grandee," she says as if a dead Company VIP was a good thing. "But who killed her?" she asks, baffled.

It's my turn to shrug. "The body hasn't been moved, although I guess these guys were in the process of doing that when the gas struck, two of them are medics. She was shot here, where she fell. Is this place significant?"

"We're close to the bridge," Hewlis answers. "But there's nothing here except system hatches. No cabins on this level."

"Mandibald could've been on her way to see the Strategist. That would explain why she wasn't at the party."

"Or she could've been heading from the bridge to

the elevator?" Hewlis adds.

"Either way, she was intercepted, and someone put a buzz-gun in her gut."

"And not very professionally," Hewlis adds. "Unless the murderer wanted the woman to suffer."

I turn on him. "And what would you know about that?"

This time, Hewlis doesn't shrug. His face shows no emotion—impossible to read. "I was a foot-soldier for a brief time during the war," he says finally. "They trained me to shoot-to-kill. To the head or chest. The gut is a sucker shot."

"That wasn't on your record," I say. I'm lying. I've no idea what may or may not be on his record. My wafer only contains the headlines.

The shrug returns. "I ain't in charge of what the Company wants to write or not write about me. But after the training, I went back to engineering. Apparently, foot-soldiers are more expendable than ship engineers."

I take another look at the body. Mandibald Glaxtinian was killed before everyone was gassed. Before the ship went into lock-down. Was her death the cause of what happened here? It's possible I suppose. One thing is for sure though, *Ariadne* didn't shoot her. I can't lay that charge at her door.

I examine the other bodies again. Medics and lower rank crew-members. I add their details to my wafer and, when satisfied, we carry on past them to the Command Floor. An expansive, curved reception area at one end of which is the bridge, closed off by a large, circular brass-like door—like some underground vault—and just as impenetrable. Five bodies lie outside. I spot the insignia of Strategist amongst the other officers.

I bring up her name on my roster.

Strategist Faraji Adebowale
Age: 31.

She's young to be a strategist, although for typical high-fliers in the Company fleet, reaching the rank of strategist before your fortieth birthday is a career must. Her career history is patchy, but this was her first ship. She's attractive… or was. Faraji Adebowale is in full dress uniform.

What was she doing up here when she should have been at the party?

Dealing with the murder, is my best guess.

I quickly tap through the other officers' info. I'm surprised to find that they have all served together before on another ship. I search their records for any other similarities but find nothing.

"Boyd mentioned that the Strategist and Professor Chandrasekhar didn't get along. Do you two know anything about that?"

A brief shake of heads. Another dead-end.

"Where's the bridge-com Drex mentioned?"

"This way." Hewlis leads me past various equipment. A laser and an arc-welding heat device. I'm no engineer, but you'd need a ship's external cannon to blast through the bridge door. The only problem? Using a laser cannon inside *Ariadne* would take out the front of the ship. These toys employed by

Drex and Hewlis wouldn't have made a scratch.

We enter an alcove with a rudimentary com, a few readout devices and a screen. I punch it into life and stare into the bridge via an internal camera. It's as Drex described it to me. What remains of the bridge crew sit slumped over in their chairs, gassed and dead, like everyone else on this goddamn death ship.

I count the bodies and, from where they sit and from what my roster tells me, I'm able to identify them. The ship's systems appear to be working without any alarms. I take a closer look at the com controls, hoping there's a record function, but the feed is live only. A simple two-way to communicate with the crew should the ship ever be in lock-down. There are other cameras on this ship, but the only way to get access to their footage would be to get access to the bridge, which ain't happening anytime soon. With *Ariadne* in lock-down, access to all coms is bridge crew only. Another security measure.

"Take me to the Hospitality Suite," I say to Velez and Hewlis. "And while we're on our way, tell me more about the other survivors. There's another three people still alive. Who are they?"

"How should I fucking know?" Velez barks, visibly agitated.

I give Hewlis a quick glance. He raises his eyebrows at me. He also seems perplexed by Velez's over-reaction.

"I'm just a third chef," Velez continues. "Remember?"

"You were up in the Hospitality Suite before you went AWOL," I say to Velez, not letting up on her. "So you must've been with them. Who are they?"

"Why not ask Hewlis?" she says.

"I'm asking you."

"No one of note," Velez says after a long pause, her mouth snatching at the air. "Although I'm sure that won't stop you barking at them."

"Who?" I repeat more forcefully.

Velez pulls a face of disgust. "There's one of those vile consorts," she says with a sneer.

"A consort?" I reply. "I suppose it's no more than I should've expected with Company grandees on board. Do you know its name? Where it's from? Who it came with?"

Velez flicks her eyes up and down, as if this line of questioning is not only pointless but irritating to her. "No," she replies. "I don't talk to that kind of filth."

I'm surprised by Velez's reaction, but her prejudice doesn't interest me. I decide to move on. "Any names for the others?"

The chef shakes her head a little too quickly.

"There's a low-level politico," Hewlis says quietly. "He's been drinking himself stupid since all this started."

"I don't want a character assassination, I just want a name," I say, irritated that Hewlis answered. My focus is on Velez.

"He is called Xev," Hewlis continues. "Xev Tranth. An aide to one of the grandees... I think."

"Xev Tranth?" I whisper. *"He's on the Ariadne?"*

The name crashes into my brain, juddering down neurones and smashing into my sensibilities. A name I'd tried to forget, to get away from. A name I hate.

Hewlis is surprised by my reaction. "You've heard of him?"

I ignore the large engineer and his over-sized face. I know Xev Tranth from back in the day. My direct superior during the goddamn war. The bastard who lied to me and the other Skilled to get us to do all those… *all those atrocities*. A hard-wired Company politico, willing to do anything, everything, and anyone to get to the top. *What the fuck is he doing here? Is he a part of this?*

"You okay?" Hewlis asks, jolting me back into the now.

My mind is a whirl, but one word he said about Xev comes to the fore. "You say he's an *aide?*"

"Yeah. Sure of it. He's been drinking ever since the gassing."

This doesn't sound like the Xev Tranth I know and hate. He was a high-flier, and then some. The presence of Xev on this out-of-control death-ship has rattled me but I'm here to do a job. And to the Skilled, the job is everything. I must remain focused. I can't let my hatred of my old boss prejudice my investigation.

"That leaves one more person," I say, trying to thrust my emotions aside.

"A waitress," says Hewlis. "One of the staff serving the party. Young and pretty."

"You have a name for her?"

Hewlis shakes his head. "She's not stopped sobbing. Someone she was close to died."

I try to take in his words, but it's difficult. Xev Tranth's name won't stop bouncing around my head. I try to push it away from me, but with the effort of holding *Ariadne's* empathic mind at bay, it's too difficult.

"Let's go meet them," I say with an irritated shake of my head. "And this time, let's take the damn elevator."

We make our way back to the centre of the ship. Hewlis pushes the elevator call button and the doors open to reveal a thin, nerdy, blonde-haired guy pointing a gun at me.

klund

I DIVE at the geek, punching him hard in the wrist. His weapon clatters to the elevator floor and he crumples, screaming in pain.

I grab the gun, and soon realise it's something else. A scientific instrument is my best guess. "Get up!" I bark.

The man stumbles to his feet, eyes wide with shock. He's young—in his twenties—his skin still glossy with youth. His blonde hair is severely-cropped so that the red of his skin shines through. His head is longer than it is wide, as if he's grown up in low gravity, yet the rest of him is normally proportioned, if not skinny. A beaky nose sits above thin, uneven lips and a weak chin, making his nose look even bigger. He's odd-looking and geeky, wearing a long lab-coat down to his knees. He rubs at his wrist with an expression like a wounded dog. "Why on earth did you do that?" he says with an annoyed squeak. "You hit me!"

"What's your name?"

He stops rubbing his wrist and sags, his tense limbs suddenly relaxing. He grabs my arm with a thin hand, a look of relief spreading over his face. "Thank space there are more survivors. I thought... that I was the only one."

"Tell me your name," I repeat, shrugging myself free.

"Eric..." the geek says, "Eric Klund."

I bring up Klund's information on my wafer.

Eric Klund.
Age: 28.
Junior Technician. Neuroteknics.

The guy has a medical career, specialising in the human nervous system, tek-implants, and cerebral enhancements. Maybe he has some answers. "What in space are you doing wandering around the ship?" I ask him. "Why didn't you report to the bridge like a good little crew-member?"

"I have been assessing *Ariadne*," Klund replies defensively, his eyes darting to the instrument I took off him. "Some of her systems have been damaged. Besides, everyone else was deceased, or so I believed." The geek looks over my shoulder at Velez and Hewlis. "I am delighted to find more survivors."

Klund talks precisely, with care taken over every syllable.

"To be perfectly honest," he continues, "I have been going a little doolally and—"

"What's this?" I hold up the device he was carrying.

"A neuro-bio scanner. Very similar to what you may find in a medibay, although this has a whole different range of calibration."

I throw the instrument over to Hewlis.

The engineer gives the device a once-over and nods.

"Please be very careful with that," Klund says. "It is an expensive piece of Company equip—" A look of shocked recognition passes over his face. "You are a… Skilled!"

"Yeah, the Company sent me to sort out this mess, which means I'm in charge."

"The Company sent you? I thought we were in hyperspace… how did you get aboard?"

"That ain't important right now. It's the *why*, you should be interested in. There was a murder before the crew was locked out of the ship's systems and everybody was poisoned." I give Klund a few moments to digest my words. "What do you know about a company Grandee who goes by the name of Mandibald Glaxtinian?" I produce my wafer and show him a 3D of the now deceased VIP.

"A murder?" The geek shakes his elongated head. "I am sadly unfamiliar with this person. I rarely get to meet anyone except my colleagues. I am just a junior."

I look at Hewlis. "Another regular grunt, huh? There's a lot of you about."

"You say she was killed?" Klund asks. "I'm shocked."

"Shot by a buzz-gun." I produce my own gun and point it at him. "Just like the one you've got concealed under your lab coat. Give it to me."

The geek reels backwards in shock and I hear Velez gasp behind me. I guess Klund thought the gun was well-hidden. But not to me. I can spot a masked piece at twenty feet, even with one eye.

Klund quickly parts the nano-fibres of his lab coat, seemingly eager to comply to my demand, and reveals the weapon strapped to his waist. He fumbles it free and passes it to me.

The gun is of unfamiliar design—old-fashioned with an ornate five-pointed star engraved on the grip and a filigree of intersecting lines artistically rendered along the barrel snub. To me a gun is a gun. You point it and create mayhem. Fancy artwork doesn't help it kill any better. "What the hell were you doing with this?" I ask, shoving it into my skinsuit.

"I found it on a member of the deceased crew." Klund hastily replies. "I've never even touched or fired a weapon in my life before." He shrugs. "I put it in my belt. I suppose it made me feel safer."

"You thought I wouldn't spot you were packing? I'm a Skilled, remember? Nothing gets past me."

"I forgot all about the awful thing," Klund replies, his voice a high whine. "To be honest, guns make me nervous. I am glad you have it now."

I'm not sure I'm convinced. The fact he was carrying a buzz-gun sure raises a few red flags over the technician.

"It is a great relief to find a Skilled aboard."

"Then help me do my job," I say, stepping up to him. "Tell me about the *Ariadne*, about what you do here."

Klund pulls himself together. "Of course," he says, his creaky voice becoming more self-assured. "I have been on *Ariadne* for just over thirteen months. My speciality is in tek-implants. Specifically, connections between organic matter and the ship's regular tek. I was not involved in any of the design aspects, or anything high-level, although I would have been thrilled to have been asked. Instead, I was brought on board to monitor how the biological and tek components of the ship interacted with one another."

"Did you notice any problems?" I ask.

"On a pioneering project like this one, there are certainly a lot of niggles and set-backs, which was very much to be expected within the parameters of—"

"I meant, any major problems with *Ariadne*. Or haven't you noticed the dead crew? Or the fact the ship is hurtling through hyperspace seemingly with no one at the helm?"

Klund swallows. "You would need to converse with Professor Chandrasekhar about those things. He oversaw the *Ariadne* project. I had nothing to do with her mind or programming. I was only responsible for the connections between organic matter and—"

"Yes, yes. What about tonight and the VIP party?"

The concept of a party seems to confuse the technician. Klund's eyebrows crease together, pinching his face, his elongated head twitching in the negative. "The event was organised by the professor. Nothing to do with me. Parties are not my thing at all. I wasn't even invited. Why would I be?"

The geek is rapidly becoming another dead end. "How'd you survive?"

"I was particularly fortunate in that regard."

"Answer the damn question!"

"I am not a fan of the regular ship air," Klund replies. "Do you have any idea of the number of bugs, particles and contaminants, including faecal matter, we inhale daily?"

The guy is starting to piss me off, but I let him continue.

"…It is quite the melting pot of disease, bacteria, and toxins. Even on a new ship like this, the air becomes quickly infested." Klund wrinkles his nose. "I try not to breathe it whenever possible. Especially when there is no reason to. I installed a simple air filtration system in my quarters. Quite ingenious, actually. It saved me. I did not know what had happened until I left my cabin and found everyone dead."

"Any ideas as to why the air was poisoned or by who?"

"It is not my place to say," Klund replies, his eyes flicking guiltily at my face—at my one good eye.

He's hiding something, but what?

"You think Professor Chandrasekhar is gonna tell you off?" I say, staring back at him so hard that he cringes. "Because I wouldn't worry about him, he's very likely dead with everyone else. Let me fill you in with a few extra details. This ship is heading on a direct line to the closest enemy territory. In under two hours, this vessel will be blown out of hyperspace— courtesy of the Company frigate that's shadowing us. Your superiors are willing to sacrifice this precious ship to prevent it getting into enemy hands. And that includes anybody left alive aboard. You get me? If you know anything that can help us stop that from happening, you need to tell me now."

"What?" The geek takes a few moments to digest

my words. "How typical of the Company. Ready and willing to destroy such a magnificent ship and all the professor's work?" Klund lets out a breath of exasperated air, the logic of the situation registering upon his thin features as a furrow of his eyebrows and the slow tightening of his jaw. "But I suppose the Company has been forced to protect its assets. It makes absolute sense."

"Right. Now you understand what we're up against, I want you tell me what it is you've been holding back from me since we started this conversation. And no bullshit."

"…It is *Ariadne,*" Klund says guiltily, his eyes narrowing. "It's very possible that she has gone insane."

cauterised

"TELL ME something I don't know," I say. "Explain to me why you think *Ariadne* is to blame for what's gone down on this ship."

Klund nods, his Adam's apple bouncing up and down. "I have no idea what went wrong with the professor's experiment." He rubs his hands together, as if he's trying to wring the words out of his long fingers. "Although I have come to the conclusion that it was *Ariadne* who gassed everyone."

"I knew it!" Hewlis says, his voice a thick, angry rasp.

"Were there any signs of odd behaviour from *Ariadne* before tonight?" I ask Klund.

The geek lowers his voice. "Professor Chandrasekhar was going to shut *Ariadne* down and start again." The words spill from Klund's mouth like a confession, his face contorted into a look of apology. "She had become irrational and argumentative."

I turn to Hewlis. "Is this true?"

The engineer performs his tell-tale shrug. "I didn't mix in the same circles as Klund. I heard nothing about any shutdown."

I stare again at the scientist. "Any idea why Professor Chandrasekhar would want to host a party of VIPs to show off *Ariadne*? Especially if she was malfunctioning?"

"Company politics are not my strong point," Klund replies. "I suppose these things are arranged weeks in advance. I have no idea about the professor's intentions. But he must have believed he had *Ariadne* under his control, why else would he have let the party go ahead?"

Klund's explanation is thin at best, except that I have experience of *Ariadne's* madness. I can feel her now, chafing away at me, writhing like a snake at the back of my consciousness. Trying to overwhelm me. It also makes sense that Professor Chandrasekhar would try and bluff his way through tonight's VIP event to keep the semblance of normality. Pretending that his Cereb-ship was functioning as expected, especially with an Arbiter like Glaxtinian aboard.

"Answer me this—is *Ariadne* capable of launching herself into hyperspace?"

The geek shrugs. "It is possible, I suppose. Her nervous system pervades into every vital system, including navigation, the Snag Drive array, her weapons and defences." Klund swallows loudly, his tongue licking at dry lips. "She is a prototype. *Ariadne* was built to test out the professor's theories. It is unlikely he would give her complete control."

"This ship ain't no goddamn prototype. Just look at her!" I reply to grunts of agreement from Hewlis. "The Company wouldn't invest in a ship like this unless they were sure everything was tried and tested."

Klund shakes his head as if dismissing a child's feeble arguments. *"Ariadne* is an empathic entity, very much like yourself. The ship, which *Ariadne's* organic matrix is an integral part of, was specifically designed to give the crew pride. Pride is an emotion an empath can pick up on. It was important to the experiment that *Ariadne* felt a sense of her own worth as she developed. A strong sense of self-esteem about who she was and what she was a part of... and of the crew that she was protecting. That is why the professor's work was so ground-breaking."

"The brain is also a Skilled?" Hewlis blurts. "Space! Just look at what your professor has done here. He's a monster!"

Klund shrugs, unfazed. "I did not design the experiment nor was I privy to its ins and outs. However, progress cannot be made without a certain amount of sacrifice."

"Well this progress you're so in favour of, nearly killed you, how does that feel?" Hewlis blurts.

Klund tries to answer. I speak over him. "How did Chandrasekhar interface with the Cereb, with *Ariadne?* Did he have a coms interface of some kind? Where is his office?"

"That I do not know," the geek replies, raising his hands as if to protect himself from my barrage of questions. "There is the main laboratory, but Professor Chandrasekhar hardly ever visited. His private office is somewhere else aboard. I don't know where. He was an intensely secretive man... but brilliant."

I bring up the ship's schematic on my mission

wafer. There's no information other than floors and cabins. Chandrasekhar's private office could be anywhere. Damn!

"Tell me, is there any way to kill *Ariadne*. Or to at least cut her off from the rest of the ship, without the professor?"

Klund shakes his head.

"But you must know something that can help us, some way to fight back against the ship?"

Klund glances over to Hewlis and the scanner he holds in his large, rough hands. "I panicked… I only did it to make sure I was safe."

"Did what?"

Hewlis nods knowingly, his thick head of grey curls bouncing around his lived-in face. "You fried the goddamn air-con system, didn't you?"

The geek sags. "I had to, I could not risk *Ariadne* gassing the ship again."

"Way to go, Klund!" the engineer says, clapping the skinny technician on the back with one enormous spatula hand. "You've just gone up in my estimation."

"I cauterised *Ariadne's* environmental controls," Klund squeaks, the words coming fast to his thin lips. "My position aboard this ship gives me access to them. I had to do it… a matter of life and death. That is why the air-con is down. Why the ship's temperature is all over the place. If we get out of this, you will tell them that, right? The Company? Make them understand?"

The admission is a hard one, shown by the pained expression creasing Klund's stretched face. It's quite a display. His act of self-preservation doesn't surprise me. If anything, it humanises the geek, but it does raise a further question.

"How do we know you didn't gas the ship in the first place? You admitted you had access."

The geek's eyes almost dart out of his face. "I would never do such a heinous thing. What would be my motive?"

I share a look with Hewlis.

"Motives are ten a penny," I reply to the scientist. "Simple revenge, anger, resentment, love, etcetera. The list goes on. What is far more important, is *opportunity*, which it appears you had in bucket-loads."

Klund shakes his head. "I had nothing to do with that. *Ariadne* did it. I'm sure of it."

"Are you just as sure the ship can't gas us again?"

The geek nods with pronounced exaggeration. "I initiated a cascade failure, resulting in the death of the air-con system. I was worried about knock-on effects to other parts of the ship. That is what I was doing when we bumped into each other. A damage assessment."

"At least we're safe," Hewlis says sardonically. "Or as safe as we can be with that other ship out there."

"Okay, Klund," I say. "What else is this ship capable of?"

"You will inform the Company I had no choice in doing what I did?" he pleads, his head bobbing up and down. "That I was trying to save *Ariadne* and the experiment?"

Velez snorts behind me. "There's nothing wrong in looking after number one," she says. "Forget the damn Company. They don't think twice about fucking us over. I have personal experience of that. You did a good thing."

I ignore her. "Sure," I reply to Klund. "If you tell me what you know about the *Ariadne*, I'll make out you're a goddamn all-round hero. Are we in any further danger from her?"

"I'm not sure," the geek replies, rubbing a hand over the blond stubble of his scalp. "She has a certain amount of independent thought, leading to independent actions."

"A goddamn accident waiting to happen," Hewlis says with a flick of his eyebrows.

"But that is how her mind was specifically designed," Klund replies to the engineer. "That was the whole point of the experiment. Battle computers are all so advanced these days that any conflict between equal numbers of opposing ships will result in a stand-off. With an autonomous entity like *Ariadne* in control, the odds of winning such a confrontation are increased exponentially. Or that was the hope. But—"

"—But something went wrong." Hewlis spits. "Of course it did."

Everyone becomes quiet, me included.

"What the fuck are we gonna do next?" says Velez, nervously breaking the silence. "We need to stop the ship, if we can't do that, we're all dead and buried."

I round on her. "We're sticking to my plan. I'm going to interrogate all the other survivors and solve the murder—I'm sure that's the link to getting out of this mess."

Velez snorts. "That's no plan, that's a death sentence!"

"Does anyone have a better idea?" I ask, eyeing Velez, the geek and Hewlis.

"Shouldn't we be looking for Professor Chandrasekhar's quarters?" the engineer says. "Shouldn't that be our priority?"

"How long do you think it would take to search every cabin and room aboard this ship?" I ask.

Hewlis draws breath to answer but I talk over him.

"Too bloody long. But let's say we're lucky and Drex and Boyd come back to tell us they've found the professor's office. He's very probably dead, gassed by his own creation. He must be, otherwise he would've done something to stop all this. And without the professor, how do we get in contact with *Ariadne?* Or destroy her? You think Chandrasekhar's data-centre would let us in just because we asked? It'd be a waste of our valuable time."

Hewlis accepts my logic with a grim nod, his mop of grey curls wriggling like a nest of worms. "You're right."

"*Drex and Boyd?*" the geek says. "There's more people alive?"

"Yeah," I reply. "And even more in the Hospitality Suite. Maybe they will have some useful information. I won't know until I go and interrogate them."

"You won't find anything of interest in Hospitality," Velez says.

"I'm a Skilled," I reply. "Brought in to discover what the hell is going on here. That's what we do— make sense of the nonsensical and find the bad guy. There's a helluva lot more going on aboard this ship than an out-of-control, insane Cereb. I'm certain of it. If not… then we're all dead. But without me, you'd be dead anyway, which means you have a simple choice: help me or get in my way—and you don't get in the way of a Skilled when he's doing his job, not unless you want to find out what it's like to be on the rough end of a buzz-gun blast." I stare at Velez, giving her time to let the threat sink in. "We're heading to Hospitality and that's final."

"Then please may I ask that you return my diagnostic scanner?" Klund asks.

"What the hell for?"

He shrugs, as if the answer is an obvious one. "I must continue my damage assessment, of course. I disabled *Ariadne's* air-con node. There may be a knock-on effect to other systems. And a cascade failure would be quite disastrous to the ship. I will finish my work as fast as I can and come and join you and the others in Hospitality."

Something about Klund, his demeanour, his need to get away grates with me. It may be the wrong decision, but I shake my head. "Didn't you hear me? We only have under two hours. Your work doesn't have priority. Besides, I want you with me. You know more about *Ariadne* than anyone else."

"But I must—"

I raise a single finger. "Hewlis, give me his scanner."

He passes it to me. I drop it to the floor and crush it under my foot. "Like I said, you're done."

Klund's hands turn into impotent fists, his face showing considerable annoyance.

"What's the matter?" I say. "You gonna report me for destroying Company property after what you did to *Ariadne?*"

"No."

"Good. Now someone hit the damn elevator button."

hospitality

WE EMERGE from the elevator and head for the front of the ship, only stopping to check the occasional body.

I'm not expecting to find any more murder victims—victims who've been shot rather than gassed—but I check them anyway. Part of me doesn't have much faith in Drex and Boyd. I'm wondering if it was a mistake to order them to search the ship. There's no way they could get access to the crew's private cabins, not without security codes, which might skew their results. Still, they are out of my hair.

My heart quickens at the thought of meeting my old boss, Xev Tranth. The fact he's aboard and still alive is something I can't ignore. The man was calculating at the very least. I'm not the type to jump to rash conclusions but I can't stop the irrational thought that I'm only aboard *Ariadne* because Xev somehow wanted me here. A ridiculous notion, but such is the power Xev once held over me.

I lead Hewlis, Velez and an agitated Klund into a long, egg-shaped oval room following *Ariadne's* artistic curves… *the Hospitality Suite*.

I am astounded. The far wall is an enormous rounded plastiglass window through which the mesmerising waves of hyperspace swirl and bubble in an iridescent display of many colours. Portholes aboard normal Company ships are a usually a thin slit of thickened, clouded glass. I've seen nothing like this before.

The interior walls have a raised complexity of brick-like shapes that flicker and dance with the flashing lights of the hyperspace display. The carpeted floor is a stylised design—a giant spider drawn in shades of red, black, and gold. *Ariadne* again. I shudder, remembering that this whole ship is one big spider and that I'm caught in its goddamn web.

Tables and chairs are strewn around inside. Some of them knocked over to hide the twenty or so bodies laid out on the floor on the far side of the room. A single occupant—a consort with bright red skin—sits on a chair, its head bowed.

I round on Hewlis. "Where the hell is everyone else?" I ask. "Xev Tranth and the waitress?"

"Drex ordered me to break into the bridge. That's where me, him and Boyd were when your pod smashed into the cargo bay. Velez was supposed to remain here," he says, looking at the chef for an explanation.

"I went for a walk to clear my head," Velez replies. "I found all the bodies in Habitation a little off-putting. Not that it helped. There are goddamn bodies everywhere. But I had to get out. Something rocked the ship, probably your arrival, and I went to investigate. As for the others? I don't know where they could've gotten to. Not my responsibility."

The chef has been annoying me ever since she turned up. "You're supposed to be a cook, so go rustle me up some food. I'm starving. The galley is next door, so you shouldn't get lost."

She stares back at me, as if the request is beneath her.

"I pistol-whipped Drex, don't make me do the same to you. And try and find something to drink. Preferably whisky."

Velez scans the room one more time, shrugs, and glides away.

"I should go as well," says Klund. "I really do need to check out the rest of the ship."

I shake my head. "You stay with me."

"But why?"

I put my face next to his. "Because you keep trying to get away."

"I just want to do my best to help out. Can't you see that?"

"And I want you to stay where I can keep my eye on you."

"You let Velez go."

"Yeah, I did, but I'm hungry and, for the moment, that's my priority."

I stride away from the annoyed geek and head towards the red-skinned consort, a hermaphroditic member of the order known as *The Jen*. It's almost naked apart from chiffon-like material covering lithe limbs, the face hidden by a pair of elegant hands tipped with long, pink fingernails. The consort hasn't moved since I entered, and if there's one thing I don't like, it's being ignored. I kick its chair with an irritated foot.

The hands drop to reveal an augmented, fur-covered face containing wide, enlarged doe-like eyes. Attentive, pointed ears flick in my direction, sitting either side the buds of two horns. Its snout is also enlarged, tipped with a black, glistening nose. Long, red, luscious hair sprouts from its head to fall over its shoulders and down its back in a cascade like a horse's mane.

A stylised, cartoonesque human antelope.

The creature is sexy… in a weird kind of way. But being exotic, attractive, and very much available—for the right price—is what the Jen are all about. They are professional companions. A polite term for *prostitute*, their bodies altered for the giving and receiving of pleasure—but they are a lot more than just playthings to be bought and then discarded.

"Who are you?" it says, the voice breathy, sensual and overtly feminine.

"I'm Vatic."

Its over-sized eyes roam across my emaciated frame, and I'm vain enough to let this bother me. I'm not in my best physical shape, that much is true.

"You're a Skilled?"

"And you're a Jen."

A snort. "Then you're like me… *not quite human.*"

I fix the creature with my good eye and reply. "I understand what it is to be different. But there is no similarity between us. You made a choice to become…" I look the creature up and down, "…*whatever that is*. I had no such luxury."

The Jen are not a separate breed like me, they are, instead, *designer-humans*. Fiercely ambitious, driven and goal-orientated—and not to be under-estimated. I tap my wafer. It reveals three consorts aboard. None of them are red-skinned. My heartbeat increases ever so slightly.

"What's your name?"

"Rooba, Rooba Jen." The Jen pushes itself up to stand on long, gazelle-like legs, its feet capped with augmented cloven hooves. Rooba is a good foot and a half taller than me. Crimson hair spills down its statuesque shoulders, glistening under the flashing lights of hyperspace. It possesses three pairs of breasts, diminishing in size above an impossibly slim waist, nipples large and pointed.

I hear Eric Klund gasp behind me. Intimate human relations are probably an unknown territory to him. Sure, I'm stereotyping the young geek, but I'm guessing the closest he's ever come to having sex is in the VR suite—and Rooba Jen is *all* sex, and pretty much nothing else, other than not-quite naked ambition.

"You're not on the Company roster," I bark. "Care to explain why?"

Rooba points towards the pile of corpses, where I spot the blue skin of another Jen.

"I came with that consort," Rooba continues. "Name of Naal Jen. There was a dropout and I was the last-minute replacement."

I take in the information with a nod of my head. That name *is* on my roster. Rooba's story sounds plausible—on the surface at least. A last-minute change could be a valid reason why Rooba is not listed, but in terms of suspects, the Jen now has a red flag hanging over its head, a flag red enough to match its bright crimson skin.

"If there's a party, there's bound to be a consort or two," Rooba continues. "I'm a Jen after all and always keen to meet new faces and people." Its eyes flick suggestively at Eric Klund. "You do understand what we are and *what we do?*"

Rooba is plying its trade, even in this goddamn horror of a situation. Something the Jen can't turn off. "Ignore it," I say to the geek. "These things are not to be trusted."

"Please," Rooba says with no trace of anger. "I may be a Jen, but I've never liked the impersonal pronoun. I'm female-preferred. With no hidden surprises… unless that's your kink."

"Female huh? I thought your kind didn't favour gender designation."

"We don't. We can be whoever or whatever you want us to be. Presently, I'm all girl." She throws back her head, emphasising her neck and boobs, a simple gesture full of practised coquettish allure.

The thing is flirting with me. I suppose that in her world, I'm quite the catch, although Rooba must know that the Skilled are not prone to attachment or emotion. *Mostly.* "You've not asked me what I'm doing here. Or how I arrived on the ship?"

Rooba shrugs again. "How should I know about any of that? Unlike you, I wasn't given a ship's roster. And who cares when you came aboard? You're a Skilled.

That makes you someone important, more important than that dim kid who put himself in charge."

I'm impressed with Rooba's faith in me although, so far, I've few clues and no suspects.

"Where were you when everyone started dying?"

The question seems to focus Rooba. "I was outside in one of the corridors," she replies, remembered horror replacing her coquettishness. "Chatting to one of the ship's command crew. Hoping to make a connection, but some onboard incident called him away."

"What kind of incident?"

"Someone had been shot. Someone important by all accounts."

I'm intrigued. Rooba is the first person I've talked to who has heard about the murder. I glance over to Hewlis and Klund who are hanging on every word the Jen says. My eye returns to the red-skinned consort and I fix her with a stare. "Yeah, I found the body," I say under my breath. "Mandibald Glaxtinian, an Arbiter."

Rooba's eyes light up. "An Arbiter? My, that would've been a catch."

"Did your mark give you any information about the victim? Or why she was shot?"

Rooba shakes her head. "We barely swapped a few words before he was called away. He collapsed seconds later, gasping for air and grasping at his throat. I went to get help, but everybody was choking… *dying* from the same thing—something nasty in the air. Then the ship jumped into hyperspace without warning. After that, I dunno. I sort of acted on autopilot. I came back here… I didn't know where else to go."

I ponder her story for a moment. It's as believable as the others I've heard. "With everyone dying, how come you survived?"

"That's easy," Rooba says, a smile of pride appearing on her elongated snout. "I grew up on one of those poisonous little colony worlds where the Company sends dumb pioneers to go and die. It was where I learnt who I was, and what I wanted to be."

The Colonies. I had a half-assed desire to go spend the rest of my days as a farmer on one of those dust-filled planets. Part of me is still attracted to that idea. The Company, in the form of Strategist StrAnng, had other plans for me.

Rooba's head lifts to look past me and through the plastiglass window, her eyes flickering with the swirls of reflected hyperspace. The red skin of her slender neck also glistens, drawing my gaze to her shoulders. I sense a strong physical urge to kiss them, to spin Rooba around. To lift its chiffon gown and to pound her statuesque ass. To feel that perfectly engineered body shuddering against me. The Jen are famous for using our desires against us. Lust, jealousy, love, and any other emotion that suits their purposes. Still, I'm impressed at the strength of my reaction. Rooba is perfectly designed, every part of it complimenting every other. A physical representation of a perfect stylised sexual allure that even I'm not immune to.

And why would I be?

I'm not human, but I still share their petty needs. If anything, the sexual responses and drives of the Skilled are more enhanced. Having full control over our bodies, over pain and pleasure receptors, and a helluva lot more, is certainly an advantage in the area of intimate human relations. It's that same control that makes me immune to her genetically-engineered charms. I find her both alluring and repugnant, but I'm digressing. "Why is your time in the Colonies relevant?"

"Because one of the first things I had augmented was my pulmonary system. Being able to filter the poisonous air, being able to breathe outside the goddamn domes was a sign of status on those backwater planets. But I was never gonna stay there. I made my escape a long time ago. I guess my enhanced lungs are why I'm still alive."

"And this job… was there anything peculiar about it?"

The Jen's long eyelashes flick in the direction of the pile of corpses.

"You know what I mean. Was anything different or unexpected?"

A shake of her head.

"Do you work at a lot of these things?"

"Yeah. Sure I do. You know how it is."

The Jen are ambitious as a breed. Desiring to fuck their way into a better life. Their goal? To become an official consort to a high-ranking politico and, more importantly, to join the elite. Wielding their power vicariously. They can be dangerous creatures. Dark, driven, sometimes malicious. Willing to do anything and anybody to fulfil their desire for power, including murder, extortion, and blackmail. And yet… the saps still fall for them. Time and time again.

"Do you know where we're going?" the Jen asks, staring back into the swirl of hyperspace. "I want to get off this ship as soon as possible."

"That's what I'm working on."

Questions still hang over Rooba, although my gut is telling me she is another dead end.

I leave the Jen and edge over to the pile of bodies. Most of them guests. Well-dressed politicos, distinguishable by their long black jackets, white shirts, and ruffles—like Mandibald Glaxtinian. There're a few waiters, crew officers and two consorts. One obese, orange-skinned with horn implants, the other lithe, blue-skinned with fish-like gills—Naal Jen—who, if Rooba is to be believed, invited her to this party. Not that the dead Jen is in any state to verify her story.

Other than the bodies, there's nothing to see. They all appear to have died the same way—gassed. I double-check their names on my roster and whistle.

Quite the VIP event.

I take a further look around, hoping to scavenge some party food, but unless I want to eat old shrimp off the floor, there's nothing. I hope Velez turns up with something soon.

I check the remaining bottles. All empty. I can't even get a damn drink. I'm about to curse in exasperation when I hear a single sob.

pirella

SITTING IN a corner behind an upturned table, I find what appears to be the nameless waitress Velez mentioned earlier. "Who are you?" I shout, rounding on her.

The girl is barely out of her teens. Long, golden-blonde ringlets surround a pointed and attractive face. One delicate hand fingers an amber pendant hung on a silver chain around her neck. Her eyes, although red-rimmed, are a mesmerising blue, staring through me as if I'm not here.

"Answer me!" I bark.

More sobs.

I kick the table aside and grab the girl by the wrist, pulling her to her feet. She's skinny—all arms, legs and tiny tits, wearing black slacks and a white server's jacket. She glances over to the corner where the bodies are laid out. Her sobbing becomes unbearable.

I punch her in the stomach, not too hard, just enough to wind her. A technique I learnt years ago. A way to focus people on me and my questions.

Behind me, I hear Hewlis grunt in protest.

The girl doubles over and retches. I drag her over to a chair and push her down, pulling up another chair to sit opposite.

Klund appears suddenly at my side, agitated and all heated up, his breath rasping.

"I do not care who you are," the geek spits. "I cannot sit back and let you treat this poor girl like this. She is obviously heartbroken."

Hewlis and Rooba also come over, staring at the girl with concern.

I pull out my buzz-gun and roughly jab the muzzle into Klund's chest. "Sit down, Eric." I say, pushing him back so that he collapses into a chair, the buzz-gun now pointing at his twitching face. "You want me to decorate the floor with your brains?"

The geek is too shocked to reply, his eyes unable to leave the muzzle of the gun.

"There's no need to behave like that," Rooba says. "Honey, *you need to calm down.*"

I sense the Jen is using some voice augmentation technique to try and manipulate my mood. "Don't play your stupid games on me, Rooba. It will take more than six tits to turn my head, so keep your snout out of my goddamn business, you get me?"

Rooba nods. All compliance and submissiveness. But I'm not fooled. Like I said, the Jen are driven, calculating and dangerous. If that is who she really is.

I turn my attention back to the waitress. "You okay?"

The young woman slowly straightens, the tears now gone. A sucker-punch to the gut will do that— and like I said, I wanted her full attention.

I grab her by the chin and lift her head up. "Tell me your name."

"Pirella," she whispers from a hoarse throat.

If she's angry about my treatment of her, it doesn't show in her tone. I tap at my wafer.

Pirella Qelline.
Age: 19.

I tap again, but that's all the info available. No digivid. Nothing. Just her name, which sounds familiar. "You're dressed as a waitress. Is that why you're here? To serve drinks?"

Pirella lifts a feeble hand and points to the body of a young kid also in a waiter's uniform.

I haul her over to the bodies, aware of Klund twitching on his chair. But he hasn't got the guts to go against me. The dead waiter looks to be in his mid-twenties, and, despite his blackened face and protruding tongue, he used to be handsome. "What was his name?"

"Denny," Pirella says, reaching out to him.

I bring up his details.

Denny Raymon.
Age: 23.
Waiter, First Class.

A digivid reveals a good-looking white kid with short black hair. There's a couple of paragraphs about his life. He worked in the hospitality industry for the last few years, rising up the ranks to end up serving grandees at functions like this. Other than one or two misdemeanours as a teenager, he's clean and was doing very well for himself… until tonight that is.

"Denny was your boyfriend, yeah?"

She nods, tears streaming down her face. "He got me this job," she replies, her voice almost a whisper.

"Waitressing?"

"Yes. He brought me aboard."

"What else?" I ask.

She says nothing and begins to sob again.

"Answer me!" I shout, convinced Pirella's grief is for real, which means she's no use to me in this state. "Or do you want me to beat up on you some more?"

She shakes her head, wiping away the tears, pulling herself together, her face full of shock and sorrow.

"Denny arranged it," she finally replies, her voice now more together. I notice it has a posh twang at odds with her job as a waitress.

"They needed extra staff for this event on the *Ariadne*. We arrived with the other waiters on the same transport. A few hours before the party began."

"Did you notice anything wrong, anything amiss with Denny, or anyone else on this ship?"

"Nothing, other than Denny was a little distracted."

"What was your job at this function? Anything more than just waitressing?"

"No… no. Of course not."

Her answer is too defensive for my liking, but without my empathy, I can't tell if she's lying.

"Go through what happened after you arrived. Step by step."

"We were brought from the surface by one of the

transports and escorted to our station by the galley. We waited there until the function started. Our job, with the two other waiters, was to serve food and drinks."

"And when people started dying?"

The look of horror returns to Pirella's face. "Denny dropped his tray. Everyone laughed and cheered but then people started choking. Collapsing. There was a smell in the air... something odd." Her eyes fall back down on to the body of her dead boyfriend.

"Focus, Pirella! You survived. How?"

"I have no idea."

I believe her. She's in shock from the deaths of Denny and everybody else, that much is for sure, but she's still hiding something from me.

I grab Pirella's wrist again and drag her over to Rooba.

"Listen up," I say to them both. "This ship is in trouble and if I don't work out what the hell is going on soon, then we'll all be dead. You two understand me?"

"We're gonna die?" Pirella says, the prospect of her own demise bringing her back to the now.

Rooba, who has been dutifully docile since my rebuke, comes alive. "Just what kinda trouble is this ship in?"

"It's not a long story. If we don't stop the ship, the Company is gonna blow it and us out of hyperspace. If either of you know anything more than you're telling me, now is the time to say. We've got just over an hour left until we all die, you get me?"

Rooba says nothing. It's hard to read emotion on

her augmented face, but I can tell the news has come as a shock to her.

"No, that can't be true," Pirella says. "It can't be."

"You think I'm lying?"

"Daddy won't let that happen." Pirella's voice is nothing more than a whisper. "He'll stop the Company. I know he will."

"Daddy?" And then I remember… *Qelline.* Of course. Another damn name from my past. "You're Ambassador Qelline's daughter?"

"Daddy will make sure no harm comes to me. You have to get a message to him."

"He won't be able to give you any help now," Hewlis says gruffly from over my shoulder.

"The engineer is right. We're in hyperspace and cut off. Tell me. What is an ambassador's daughter doing waitressing on a ship like this?"

"I can vouch for the girl…"

I whip around to see Velez holding a plate with various cured meats, sliced bread and cheeses.

"Her ambassador father gave her clearance to come aboard," she continues. "He's some big cheese with the company. Denny, her boyfriend, told me all about it. I've worked with him before."

"You were reticent to talk about the survivors last time I asked," I say to the chef. "Particularly this girl. What changed?"

Velez shrugs.

"Is this true, Pirella?"

The girl nods but doesn't break eye-contact with the chef.

I grab Pirella by the chin, forcing her attention

back on to me. "Listen up and listen well. If you want to get off this death ship and see your father again, you need to tell me everything, understand?"

Pirella draws breath to reply but is interrupted by a loud shout from the doorway.

I turn to see Drex and Boyd entering the Hospitality Suite, dragging a body behind them—a body unlike anything I've seen on this ship so far…

blank

DREX AND Boyd unceremoniously dump a lump of bloated and formless flesh on the Hospitality Suite carpet.

"What the hell is that?" Hewlis shouts.

"That's what we want the Skilled to answer," Drex replies.

The thing is an unnatural white colour and roughly the size of a man. More like a beached albino whale than anything human… but that's what it once was.

I grab a handful of cheese, meat and bread off Velez's plate, pushing them together to make a crude sandwich and go look.

The thing stinks and stinks bad. But the smell ain't that of decomposition. It's sickly and sweet. Not exactly putrefaction but some other degenerative process, although it's halted or at least stalled. There's a definable head, torso and legs, all merged into one formless mass. The flesh is pallid, jelly-like and translucent, except where it's been torn and scuffed from being dragged through the ship. Just what were Drex and Boyd thinking?

"It smells," Pirella says, sharing a nervous glance with Velez.

I crouch down to get a closer look, taking a bite out of my makeshift sandwich. Behind me, I hear Pirella gag. I take another bite and suddenly I'm ravenous. I glance up at Rex and Boyd. "Where did you find this thing?"

"We were being thorough, like you ordered," Drex replies, unable to hide his scorn. "Searching the maintenance decks. The area is hardly visited. Full of automatic systems. But we checked anyway. We'd just finished inspecting one of the supply areas when…" Drex swallows loudly.

"When what?" I run my hand over the pallid flesh. It's still warm.

"We saw a line of pink froth," Boyd says. "Dripping from a broken hatch. Drex went to investigate and—"

"—And that thing dropped on me," Drex finished. "Nearly scared us both to death."

"Did you find anything on the body or near to it?" I ask. "Any ID?"

"Body?" Hewlis says, as if suddenly waking up. "You mean… this thing was once human?"

"Yeah," I reply, letting that information sink in, casting my eye over the other survivors to see if anyone is less surprised than they should be. They all seem equally shocked and appalled. "Answer my question," I say, turning back to Drex.

"We found nothing," the kid replies. "No clothes or belongings… just some kind of dissolved biological matter—that pink froth Boyd mentioned. That's why we brought it straight here."

"Which is just about the dumbest thing you could've done," I bark. "You should've left it in situ and come and got me. Who knows what evidence you've destroyed?"

"We thought you'd want to see it straightaway," Boyd says.

"That's right, but I didn't want you to drag the thing all over the goddamn ship!"

A familiar face appears in the doorway, and I'm unprepared for it. A man I haven't seen in years. A bastard going by the name of *Xev Tranth*.

I have a sudden vision, a sharp memory etched into my mind—the last time I saw him. My old boss leaning over his desk, resting on twin fists, his face twisted into anger, shouting at me. An argument over the double-agent, Esta. The only woman who's ever been able to get to me. The woman he ordered me to kill. I shot Esta dead with my buzz-gun. And I've been punished for that decision every goddamn day of my life since.

The memory rocks me, knocks me sideways. I take a deep, calming breath and push those feelings aside. Instead, I concentrate on who I am. On Vatic. On my skills and focus on assessing him...

Xev has aged poorly. The skin of his face is flaccid, fitting badly around his eyes and chin, bulging on his cheeks, creating twin shadows, pock-marked and tired looking—the obvious result of a failed juvo-treatment or two. He reminds me of those century-old digivid show hosts—living mummies only held together by their intense desire for ageless youth. His artificial cheekbones are framed by absurd long hair in a style that should belong to an adolescent, not a man in his early sixties. His pallor is more orange than pink, the skin puffy and blemished. Xev is also painfully thin, probably from the overuse of stims, or he's had his gut rewired. He's dressed for the party, a thick purple velvet dress-coat and ruffles. A pair of absurd cowboy boots completes his look. Xev was always a dandy. Even during the war, he wore his uniform with a flourish. But the proud, powerful and ambitious Company executive I once knew is now nothing more than a loose collection of bones and sallow flesh…

The man has gone to seed.

His eyes light up when he sees me, his mouth opening to speak, but I don't want to talk to him. Not yet. *Not ever.* Although I realise that won't be possible.

"Vatic!" he blurts, pushing past Drex and Boyd, heading straight for me.

I brace myself for a tirade of abuse. The man, apart from hating everything and everybody, had reserved a particular hatred for the Skilled, and especially for a Skilled named Vatic.

"Thank the gods!" he says.

I feel a sudden urge to straighten my back and to salute. Back in the day, following orders was important to me. That, and the concept of command. Thankfully, I grew up, like all the Skilled.

"This is Vatic!" he slurs, and I realise he's drunk. "The finest Skilled I ever worked with. The fucker is a bona-fide marvel… if you can call his breed men."

He laughs at what he thinks is a rather clever witticism, but everyone remains silent, their eyes fixed on the body-blank lying on the floor. He sticks out a hand for me to shake.

Even though I hated who he was and what he stood for, Xev was also one of the most driven humans I've ever met. *Why is he being friendly? This is not the Xev Tranth I once knew. Gone is his sense of unchallenged superiority. In its place is something reduced… lacking.* I can't pretend that I'm not pleased at this change. I disliked his methods and his ethics. He was one of those Company bastards that lied to me and the other Skilled. Convincing us that what we were doing in the war was right. I can't fully blame him for everything. *We were all complicit.*

"I've seen something like this before," I say, ignoring Xev's outstretched hand and pointing at the body.

"What the fuck?" Xev blurts, noticing the lump of sallow, white flesh for the first time.

"This person was killed and injected with nanites designed to remove all ID markers," I continue, speaking to everyone. "DNA, gender, race, facial features, teeth and stature have all been erased… nano-degenerated. Given enough time, it would've been totally broken down."

Xev unceremoniously kicks at the body with his foot. "I ain't seen one of these things since the war. Looks recent. But it could be up to three or four days old. Jeez!"

"And what makes you such an authority?" Klund asks.

Xev shrugs. "Like I said, it's from the war. The temporary replacement tek the Company developed back then."

"But why would someone do that?" Rooba asks, her doe eyes flicking between me and Xev, sensing the tension between us.

"That's very simple, my pretty," Xev replies, his voice full of malicious glee. "Someone on this ship has been replaced." He winks at me. "Someone here isn't who they say they are. Isn't that right, Vatic?"

replaced

"WHAT DO you mean *replaced?"* says Hewlis. "I don't get it."

"It's simple," I explain. "Like Xev said… the tek responsible for creating this body-blank comes from the war. Illegal then, and illegal now. Used by covert agents to gain entry to enemy bases, ships and compounds."

I straighten up, annoyed to find that I'm still shorter than my old boss.

"All they need is a basic DNA profile of the victim," I continue, "with a physical and facial match, usually someone of similar build and sex, and the nanite tek mimics them. A passing likeness enough to fool most people not paying that much attention. Their victims were usually killed and dumped. And if hiding the body wasn't feasible, the tek could blank them, making ID impossible, gaining the agent valuable time. Which is what I believe has happened here. The technique was never used for deep cover though. Usually for an 'in and out' attack or recon mission. And with nanites, there's always complications. An extreme measure taken by someone desperate, or on a suicide mission. But the war was many years ago. The tek may have progressed in that time."

Drex runs a hand through his thick, greasy hair. "You mean there really is an imposter aboard?"

I feel Xev's eyes boring into me. "Yeah," I reply.

"And it could be one of us?" Velez asks, staring around the room, her neck twitching almost continuously.

Pirella can't seem to take her wide eyes off the body-blank. "But who would do that and why?" She's shares another glance with Velez, as if she's expecting the chef to know the answer. "It's disgusting."

Even with her face all puffy and her blond curls sweaty and matted, Pirella is pretty. The kind of beauty her ambassador father no doubt paid for. It's a professional job only noticeable if you know what you're looking for. Her skin has a slight plastic quality. Her face doll-like. Pirella is augmented but, unlike Rooba, Pirella would be difficult to copy. Some of the girl's augmentations may not be DNA-based. Making it hard for the replacement tek to replicate her as she is today—but the tek could've been honed many times since the war. I decide to keep Pirella on my suspect list... with everyone else.

"I'm not sure," I reply. "As for motive? I'll tell you that when I find out who they are."

Drex speaks up. "But we're still heading for rival space. And whoever it is will die with the rest of us when we get there..."

I see the cogs slowly turning in Drex's mind, as he makes the obvious conclusion.

"…Unless they are responsible for jumping *Ariadne* in the first place," he says.

"That's right, soldier," I reply, pleased that Drex is coming around to my way of thinking. "It may be possible the imposter died with the rest of the crew, but I doubt that very much. I need to identify the phony and identify them fast, because when I do, I'll be in a better position to understand what's going on here. And maybe, just maybe, we can get ourselves out of this situation." I let the words hang for a few seconds.

Xev takes his dazed attention away from the body. "Situation? What the hell are you all talking about?"

"The ship is heading for enemy space," Velez replies, her voice stressed into a high-pitched whine.

"Shit! I take it the Company ain't gonna let that happen, huh?" Xev replies, his booze-addled mind still agile enough to put two and two together.

"But you can stop that, can't you?" Pirella asks me, her head bobbing on a slender neck. "You can get us out of this?"

Xev takes a swig from a hip flask and grimaces. "How long do we have?"

I glance at my wafer.

22:37

"Just under an hour and a half."

"Well ain't that the fucking biscuit!" Xev says. "I knew this party was going to be a bust."

"If you ain't got anything positive to add, shut your mouth!"

"Maybe I do know something," Xev says, the skin of his ruined face stretching oddly. "I'm not sure where this fits into the general sense of what the fuck is going on, but when I was on my way back here, I'm pretty sure I saw someone lurking in one of the side corridors. I called after them, but they melted into the shadows. Scared the bejesus out of me, if I'm honest. I didn't see a face. But it was a guy, I'm sure of it. Thickset, short, with silvery hair. I thought it might be Chandrasekhar, but it was just a glimpse."

"The professor?" I bring up a digivid of Chandrasekhar on my wafer. "It can't be him. He favours Indian ancestry. Is thin and bald."

I show the digivid to Xev who shakes his head. I then perform a filter search and get no matches. "There's also no one aboard matching that description. Whoever you saw, they're not on the ship's roster. Unless you were mistaken."

Xev raises his hands, placing one on his chest. "That's what I saw. Hand on heart."

"Where was this?"

"Not far away. I was toddling back from one of the cabins. Terrible stink of burnt meat. Made me want to chuck."

"Where we found the fried bio-systems," Hewlis says, narrowing his eyes at Klund.

I let my hand fall onto the stub of my holstered buzz-gun. "Either Xev was seeing things, or there's an extra person aboard who shouldn't be."

"Hey! I may be one or two sheets to the wind, but I know what I saw."

Xev Tranth is a wreck of his former self, but the

man was always the straight-as-a-die type, unless he had a reason to lie.

"If there's a stowaway aboard," Klund says, his voice whining, "I think we should go find them at once."

His words are followed by murmurs of agreement.

I raise my hand. "What you think we should or shouldn't do is irrelevant. I'm in charge, remember?" I turn my attention back to Drex. "You. Did you complete the roster as ordered?"

Drex shakes his head. "There's no way we could check cabins and other parts of the ship that are off-limits. We started at the bottom deck and were making our way up when we stumbled onto this." He motions towards the mound of blubbery flesh on the floor. "We brought it here and gave up on the body count."

I'm annoyed with Drex and let it show. I expected him to do as he was ordered, but the kid likes to buck authority. I turn to face everyone. "An imposter is either at large somewhere else in the ship or right here in this room with us. My gut is telling me it's one of you. You might as well reveal yourself now, because I'm gonna winkle you out one way or another…"

Xev claps his hands in a show of delighted applause, whilst Eric Klund, who has been sitting next to Pirella, jumps to his feet, obviously annoyed. "What makes you so frigging sure he is one of us?" he bleats like a chastised child.

"He? I repeat," rounding on him. "You know his gender?"

"Don't play word games," Klund says, his voice an

annoyed screech. "I meant he, she…" He gives Rooba an apologetic look. "… Or it."

I ignore the geek. "Did you or Boyd see anything out of the ordinary while you were searching the ship?"

Drex shakes his head. "Not as such, but…"

"But what?"

Drex looks at Boyd for support. "I dunno… I kinda felt like we were being watched."

Boyd nods his head. Whatever grief he may have been feeling the last time we met, seems to have been buttoned down. "Yeah, down on the deck where that thing was hidden. I sensed it too. And I thought I heard breathing. Heavy, rasping breath."

"If you were being watched, why didn't you mention it before?"

"We couldn't be sure," Boyd replies. "We didn't actually lay eyes on anybody."

I wonder if Boyd and Drex, and maybe Xev, are suffering from the telepathic barrage coming from *Ariadne's* mind. I'm not human, I don't know how resistant they are to her, but my bet is that it's making everyone a little paranoid. "Forget it," I say. "Do you have anything else to report?"

The low-rankers look at one another.

"Out with it!"

"The door to Hydroponics," Drex begins.

"Go on."

"It was broken."

Boyd nods at his side.

There's one thing about Company ship design, and it's no different, even on an advanced ship like the *Ariadne*—hatches. They are sturdy, each built to resist depressurisation and any number of other shipboard emergencies. What Drex is saying doesn't make sense. "What do you mean *broken?*"

"Like something was trapped inside and broke its way out."

I don't like the sound of that," Hewlis says, his eyes darting to the entrance and beyond.

"Don't make assumptions!" I bark at Drex. "Was there any evidence of an explosion?"

The two kids glance at each other again. This time, it's Boyd who speaks, his head shaking. "The door was bent outwards, like it had been hit with a battering ram."

"Are you deaf? No more goddamn assumptions! Okay?"

The kid flinches at my words, but nods.

"Where's Hydroponics?"

"Bottom deck."

I bring up *Ariadne's* schematics on my wafer. Hydroponics stretches the full length and width of the ship. Too large for a small vessel like this one— maybe it has another function? It will have to wait. "I'm gonna take a look where Drex and Boyd found the body blank," I say, making a quick decision. "Hopefully, they missed something. Then I'll examine the door to Hydroponics."

"And what about the rest of us?" Klund says.

"You're coming with me," I reply, finishing the remains of my makeshift sandwich. "All of you. No one is leaving my sight until this is over and done with. Oh... I almost forgot. There's one more thing that I need to deal with." I pull my buzz-gun and point it at Boyd and Drex. "Give me your weapons…"

xev

"*WHAT THE* hell!" Drex shouts.

"That's a direct order, soldier!" I bark at him. "There's no way I'm letting a possible imposter run around this ship with a loaded rifle. You get me?"

"But what if you're the imposter?" Drex replies weakly, looking around for support.

"And how do you figure that?" Hewlis says. "You were there when Vatic arrived. You left him in the airlock to die, remember? He's the only guy on this death-ship we *can* trust... or are you too stupid to realise that? Do as Vatic says and give him your guns."

Drex baulks at the engineer's words, but Boyd doesn't need any more encouragement. He passes his rifle to me.

I turn to Drex. "Your turn, soldier, or you end here."

"You really think it could be me?" Drex says. "Boyd knows me better than anyone. Isn't that right?"

"Give it up, Drex," Boyd replies. "Hewlis is bang on the money, there's no way Vatic is the replacement. We gotta trust him."

Drex sags. Hewlis steps forward and grabs the gun off Drex. The kid lets him take it, but he ain't happy.

I remove the charges from both guns and stamp on them, the units smashing.

"Well that's just great!" Drex says. "What if we needed those later?"

I ignore him and turn to the rest of the survivors. "We're gonna pair up to keep a close eye on one another. Hewlis, you're with Klund." I turn to the Jen. "You go with Pirella. Which leaves Velez and Xev Tranth. Drex and Boyd can lead the way."

Boyd is the first to move, pulling Drex with him. He glances at the body-blank. "You sure it's okay to leave that behind?"

"It's dead," Xev announces. "The poor fucker ain't going nowhere, whoever it was."

"Get moving," I say. "And keep your partners in sight at all times."

We leave Hospitality and head for the centre of the ship.

Suddenly, Xev is at my side. "Are you ignoring your old boss?"

I resist the urge to punch him in the guts, although I decide to keep this as a real possibility if he irritates me any further. But he's right. If I'm gonna do this properly, I'm gonna have to talk to the bastard. I make a show of looking at my wafer and bringing up his details.

Xev Tranth.
Age: 63.
Junior Diplomatic Aide.

I let a smile twist my lips. Hewlis told me Xev was a low-level politico, which I found hard to swallow, but the engineer was right. The man has been demoted to a junior.

"Is it all there?" Xev asks. "The fall from grace of Xev fucking Tranth in goddamn Company black and white?"

The information on Xev is patchy at best. "What happened?"

"You don't know?"

"Just answer the goddamn question."

Xev takes a long breath and shakes his head. "You, more than most, understand what the Company is like, factions constantly vying with each other for power and influence? During the war, those factions were forgotten, and we all pulled together. Afterwards and victorious, those same factions emerged again to take part in a grab for power. Unfortunately, I chose the wrong side."

"Ouch."

"It wasn't like me to lick the wrong ass-hole, but the war had me all fired up. My big play to get on the new Executive fell flat on its arse. I was lucky to escape with my life."

"You were always a survivor."

"You and me both. I was reconciled to finding myself on the wrong end of a buzz-gun, like most of the other 'conspirators', as we were called. Surviving was one of the most unpleasant experiences of my life, but here I am."

"What's a junior diplomatic aide doing attending a VIP party on a ship like this?"

Xev takes a hefty swig from his hip flask. "Ever since my fall from grace, I've been working on my glorious return. I stumbled onto the *Ariadne* project accidentally. My plan was to get myself aboard and suck up to Professor Chandrasekhar. I did my research on that fucking bastard and then some. I've known about him since the war. He's a genius amongst many other talents, but geniuses often have flaws. The professor is fiercely narcissistic and loves nothing more than to be told how wonderful his work is. My intention was to play on this vanity and wheedle myself into this or his next project."

"How is that going?" I ask with a malicious tone.

Another sigh let out through his lips in a long hiss. "I don't have the luck I used to have. I made one goddamn mistake, and only just escaped with my life. And here I am forced to come begging cap in hand to some narcissistic twat. Look at the fucking mess that turned into." He raises the flask to his lips. "Cheers!"

I snatch it away before he can take a swig.

"Hey!" he complains.

The flask is nearly full. I sniff the contents. Brandy and expensive at that. As far as I remember, Xev always had expensive tastes. Judging by the look of him, he has downed more than a sip or two. "You're drunk. How come this ain't empty?" I ask.

He throws a lazy finger at the brandy. "That's what I was doing before I returned to Hospitality. Refilling my flask. If we're all gonna die on this fucking death ship, I thought things would go better with a little drinkie or two."

"Where did you get it?"

"I pilfered it from one of the cabins," he says conspiratorially.

We pass a group of bodies lying on the floor and his eyes linger on them with a bleakness that surprises me. Xev was never one to baulk at death. If anything, he revelled in it. Maybe his fall from power, his botched juvo-treatment, and his resultant alcoholism has mellowed the guy? "So how come you're not also lying on the floor with the recently deceased?" I ask him.

He shrugs drunkenly, while sticking out his bottom jaw, the skin of his face stretching peculiarly. "I dunno. I was mingling with one of the consorts when it started coughing and fell over, gasping for breath—the large orange one—I like them with a bit of weight on their bones, if you remember?"

"Just tell me how you survived," I demand.

Xev smiles. "It's sure good to see you again."

"This ain't a class reunion," I bark. "I'm working. Tell me!"

He nods, the smile staying in place. "There was a strange smell in the air that burned my throat, like shorting electronics or ozone mixed in with shit. I noticed everyone coughing and gasping and other guests collapsing. I covered my mouth and nose with a serviette and splashed it with brandy from my flask."

Xev's story ain't particularly believable, but then again, it's similar to all the other stories I've been told so far, and they can't all be lying. I put the flask to my lips and take a swig. The brandy is a fine blend. It falls into my stomach with a pleasant warmth. Personally, I prefer whisky—a buzz-gun to the gut rather than a stroke of a feather. I let the spirit sit there, allowing it to seep slowly into my system. "Nice," I say. "But brandy ain't my style. You tell me you researched the professor… what did you find out about him?"

Xev's eyes narrow. "Don't you have it all in that wafer of yours?"

"There's not much to go on. Some big cheese with too much power and no moral sense. Sounds like a regular Company bastard."

"Oh, this is just too damn delightful," Xev says, chuckling to himself. "But then again you Skilled were never interested in where you came from, were you?"

"What do you mean?"

Xev pulls himself up to his full height and beams down at me. Upon the loose skin of his face, the expression is nightmarish. "Chandrasekhar is your family. Well as near to blood that you damn mixed-breeds can get."

I take in the words with little emotion. The Skilled were another Company experiment. One that was originally banned. The closest I ever came to kin was sharing a ghetto with all the other genetic rejects back in Internment. "What do you mean by that?"

"I mean… *he's your father.* Or at least one of them. Not literally, of course, but he was part of the team that singled out the empathy gene and the few other traits that they illegally crammed you with."

"You're right, I've never been concerned with where I came from," I say. And it's true. I'm alive and a Skilled—that's enough to contend with. "You think I don't know that my breed was manufactured?" I tell him. "Born out of a Company experiment? That's nothing new to me. So Chandrasekhar created the Skilled," I reply. "I suppose that makes sense when you see what he was trying to do with this ship."

"The professor likes to keep his dirty secrets... *secret*. Turns out, Chandrasekhar was the only survivor of the team that created you. Which is suspicious in itself. It was difficult to piece together information about the man as the professor is intensely private. He has no friends or lovers... just his pets."

"Whatever is programmed into my genes doesn't stretch to caring about my past," I spit. "I'm a man of little emotion. Other than self-pity. The bastard was a part of my creation, just as he was a part of *Ariadne*— both are flawed and very dangerous designs."

"Ain't they just!"

I decide to cut through Xev's bullshit. "How did you get aboard exactly? Did Chandrasekhar invite you?"

"Him? Hell no. He has no idea who I am or that I even exist... which is what I was hoping to change tonight. He had a lot of power in the Company. I pulled in the last of my favours. Tonight was make or break."

"I suppose that makes sense," I reply, a malicious grin on my lips. "I wondered what a washed-up loser was doing at tonight's VIP event..."

The drunken smile that has been plastered on Xev's face since we started this conversation suddenly disappears, replaced with the familiar sneer I've seen countless times before, even if it is hidden behind the many folds of his juvo-mangled face.

"You're sure enjoying my fall from grace, aren't you?"

"If that's what it is."

"Hell, I wish I was here as part of some clever plan." Xev sighs, the breath leaving his body like a deflating balloon. "But I'm not lying, and you know it."

"That's what I'm here to find out. And *I always get the guy.*"

"You were always a cocky fucker. You and that partner of yours, Esta. You were my most effective operatives."

"Don't you dare mention her name!" I shout at him, aware of everyone looking at me.

"Well that sure touched a nerve."

"Shut up and get out of my sight!"

"Now why would I do that? Haven't you figured it out yet? Sometimes you Skilled miss the bleeding obvious."

"Figured what out?" I snap back at him, wishing I hadn't let the man talk to me. He brings back far too many painful memories.

"Isn't it obvious to your brilliant, analytical mind? …I'm the only guy aboard this hell ship who you *can* fully trust." He makes a grab for the brandy flask and I'm too shocked to stop him taking it off me.

He's right. Xev hasn't been replaced, that's for sure. He is who he says he is. His confidence with me comes from our association during the war. If he was lying, I'd spot that in him a mile off, empathy or not. I pull a grim smile… "Shit!"

"Looks like the old team is back together." Xev

takes a large swig of brandy, winks, and goes back to walk with Velez, just as Pirella screams.

keycard

I TURN to see Pirella holding her hand to her mouth, while she and Rooba are staring down a darkly-lit side corridor.

I stride over to her. "What's the girl screaming about?" I say, looking at the Jen for explanation.

"She saw something."

"Saw what?"

Pirella tries to speak through her sobs, but her words are incomprehensible.

I clench my fist. "Do you want another sucker punch to the gut?"

Pirella shakes her head, wiping her tears away. "It was a boy," she says, regaining her composure. "A boy with the face of an old man and silvery hair watching me with hateful eyes."

I share a glance with Xev. "Ain't that what you saw, silvery hair?"

Xev takes a swig from his flask and nods.

"Did anyone else see or hear anything?"

The reply is a series of shaking heads.

"Those eyes…" Pirella says, tears forming in her

own red-rimmed blue eyes.

"What about them?"

"They were evil, staring… full of loathing."

"A boy you say? Are you sure?"

"He was in the shadows."

I walk past Pirella and into the darkened corridor. Nothing. But I believe the girl. With her and Xev seeing the same thing, I have to conclude that there is someone or something out there watching us. Unless she's trying to play me for a sap.

"What was he wearing?"

"I only saw his face," Pirella replies. "He ran away as soon as I screamed."

"Ran away?"

Pirella ignores me, her eyes still staring down the corridor.

I hold up my wafer, its light illuminating the girl's face. "From now on, everybody keep an eye out for anything suspicious. For anybody watching or following us… stay vigilant."

"Great," Drex spits. "And what are we supposed to do if there is someone out there who has it in for us? Wave them away? You took our guns, remember?"

Drex has a point. But I'm a lot happier, knowing the twitchy kid doesn't have his hands on a rifle.

We continue to the centre of the ship. After Pirella's screaming, everyone is on edge. I decide against using the elevator and we head down the stairwell past a few floors to the lower decks. The light here is more subdued, emphasising that this area is not regularly visited. I'm impressed to see the ship design has not been diluted. It is beautiful from top to bottom, despite *Ariadne* lurking behind its manicured facade. She is still pushing at my mind, trying to find a way in. I can resist her, but not for long. Luckily, I only have an hour and a half left to solve this thing, any longer and *Ariadne* might break through my defences.

After crossing a few more intersections, Drex leads us to a small pentagonal chamber with a high ceiling at the end of a cramped corridor.

Service panels line the segmented walls. A control monitor blinks and crackles, its screen cracked. Various readouts now unintelligible. Something heavy must have hit it to smash the almost unbreakable glass. High above, further than anyone could reach without assistance, is an open panel stained with the pink froth Boyd mentioned earlier. A ventilation shaft of some kind.

I take out my wafer and check the ship schematics. "A service area," I announce. "And well out of the way. Luckily, you were ordered to search the ship, otherwise it would've never been found… Whoever put the body up there didn't expect it to be discovered any time soon. But the big question is… *how?*"

I turn to Hewlis. "What kind of lifting equipment does the ship have?"

The engineer begins to hunch his shoulders.

"And if you shrug at me one more time, I'll break your damn neck!"

Hewlis stops in mid-movement, his shoulders carefully dropping. "I would imagine the grav would be turned off in these areas when inspection was needed," he says.

"Which means anyone could've dumped the body.

Get over here. I'm gonna need a bunk-up."

Hewlis lumbers over and links his hands. I put my foot in them and he hoists me up to the ventilation shaft. A quick look tells me the inspection panel has been wrenched open. The lock twisted and broken… There's no marks or scratches to indicate a tool had been used and, if I didn't know any better, I'd say the cover panel was ripped away by powerful hands. According to Drex and Boyd, the hatchway to Hydroponics was 'broken' from the inside. I think back to the apparition Pirella and Xev saw. Could there be a monster loose on the ship? If so, what the hell did it have to do with the body-blank? I admit it, I'm a little freaked by this development. For now, though, all that concerns me is evidence. Speculation will get me nowhere.

"What do you see?" Drex asks from below.

I ignore him, pulling myself upwards to clamber into the tight ventilation shaft. Apart from a whole load of sticky goo, the shaft is empty. I'm about to drop back down when I spot something poking out of a joint between the piping that runs the length of the shaft. I pull it free and recognise it immediately. It's part of a rectangular temporary keycard issued to those new aboard ship, used before their cabin's information can be programmed to their bio-ident. It's made of clear crystal imprinted with the same relief I saw in the cargo bay—a giant stylised spider sitting within its web, although it's snapped in two. Half of the card is missing. I wipe it clean on my skinsuit and reveal a code.

At last… *a damn clue.*

I drop back down and re-examine the card fragment in the light of the inspection room.

"What's that?" Klund asks, keen to see.

I hold it up so that everyone can look. "It's a pass key." I give it to Klund, who almost snatches it off me.

The guy is becoming a real pain, but I have other concerns. I access the ship schematic, enter the code and find the room in question. It's located on the first habitation deck—where the Strategist and her superior officers would've been quartered. The keycard belongs to an important ship-board person. But who? My theory that one of the survivors was the imposter is suddenly put into doubt. None of them would be quartered in such an important area, or not at all—as in the case of Xev, Rooba and Pirella the waitress, who were temporary guests at the party.

There are only two explanations… the keycard doesn't belong with the body-blank or someone else was replaced. Someone who we've not yet found. I'm perplexed. This investigation is throwing up more damn questions than solutions. I decide to do what I always do in these situations. To concentrate on my inquiry. To gather as many clues as I can before the time runs out.

The others also examine the card, except Velez, Pirella and Rooba, who seem disinterested in my discovery. Either due to guilt or something else. Without my empathy, I'm as blind as I was back in the Zeta-Karst Laboratories. I'm thinking that I should force them all to look, but that idea is cut short.

Xev looks me straight in the eye. "This comes from the same cabin where I stole the brandy from," he says, his badly-aligned eyebrows struggling to rise on the tight skin of his forehead. "It belongs to that jumped-up bitch, Mandibald Glaxtinian."

guns

"YOU WHAT?" Boyd says, squaring up to Xev.

My old boss gives the blonde kid a confused look. "I'm just saying that I know who owns this keycard. A Company grandee I've heard of before. A real piece of work. What's that to you?"

A shocked look crosses the blond kid's face, like he can't believe what Xev has just told him. "You mean that thing we found here, that blob, was… _was her?_"

I shake my head. "No, I don't think so. Unless the replacement-tek used to create the body-blank has advanced significantly since the end of the war, Glaxtinian couldn't have been replaced. I already found her body up by the bridge. Murdered by a buzz-gun to the gut. If she'd been the imposter, her corpse would've reverted to its original form or showed signs of nano-degeneration. The nanites get their energy directly from living cells. It's not Glaxtinian."

"She was murdered?" Boyd whispers.

"That's why I was brought aboard, to solve this murder and to stop this ship. Or haven't you been listening? I thought that between you and Drex, you were the one with the brains. Don't start proving me wrong."

Boyd's chin drops to his chest. What's wrong with the kid?

"What I don't understand," Hewlis says, his booming voice filling the small chamber, "is why Glaxtinian had a cabin at all. She was a party guest, not a member of the crew."

"That's irrelevant!" Klund replies, throwing his hands up in the air in exasperation. "If you are sure the body-blank isn't Glaxtinian, then we're no closer to finding out who it is, are we?"

I ignore the whining scientist. "I've no idea why Glaxtinian's keycard was found with the body-blank. Unless it was put there deliberately to throw us off the investigation. I doubt that. The body was hidden clumsily—it would've been found sooner or later. But whoever hid it didn't expect it to be discovered so quickly. I'm sure of that. And they didn't reckon on having a Skilled aboard either." I smile. "I'm quite the spanner in the works. Hewlis is right. I assumed Glaxtinian was just another guest aboard the *Ariadne*, on board for the party and nothing more. The keycard tells another story—she was here to stay."

I turn my attention to Xev. "How did you know Glaxtinian had a cabin?"

My old boss smiles. "The same transport brought us both from the planet, including all her luggage. She was too high-ranking to chat to me, of course, made a point of ignoring my polite attempts at conversation. I wasn't surprised, she has quite the reputation for being an arrogant bitch. When we disembarked, the ship's bursar gave her a keycard and arranged for her things to be picked up and taken to what I assumed was her cabin. I noticed a few likely-looking cases being unloaded in the cargo bay and, as I'm one to not miss an opportunity…"

"You broke in to a ship's cabin?" says Klund, who's nerd gene is finding the information harder to swallow than murder. "The doors are impassable once locked."

"Obviously not," Xev says, producing his brandy flask and toasting everyone before taking a swig. "Glaxtinian brought some top-class booze aboard. And why shouldn't I steal off the bitch? She was never gonna help me get anywhere."

"Answer Klund's question," Hewlis says with a hint of aggression. "How did you get into her cabin without a key?"

Xev smiles. "There isn't any door I can't crack, isn't that right, Vatic? *Ariadne* might be impressive, but the tek controlling the doors is the same as every other shit-hole ship in the Company."

"That is a serious offence!" Klund continues, his eyebrows furrowing like warring caterpillars.

Xev gives him a showman's bow. "I haven't lost my touch… I've said it before and I'll say it again, never under-estimate Xev Tranth."

My old boss came from poor beginnings on some forgotten backwater planet. A place where he survived on his quick wits and his equally quick fingers—a story he often recited to me—as if I ever gave a shit. But that was Xev all over, a loud-mouthed braggart.

"Hand it over," I say and Xev passes the card to

me. "And that's not all—give me the flask."

"What?" he replies like a wounded dog. "Why?"

"Because I need you sober." I give him an expression that tells him I'm not to be disobeyed and the man reluctantly passes me the brandy.

My next move is a calculated one. I pull out the decorated buzz-gun I took off Eric Klund and offer it to Xev.

My old boss stares back at me with a confused expression on his face.

"Take it."

"How come he gets a gun?" Drex says angrily. "The man's a goddamn drunk."

"You're right, of course," I reply to him, wondering when this kid's mouth will ever stop running away with itself. "But I know Xev. I've worked with him before. Sure, he's half-cut and a full-time prick, but he's not been replaced that's for sure. All my instincts tell me he's the only one of you losers that I can trust. So he gets the buzz-gun. And besides, there could be something out there. With two of us armed, our odds are improved by one-hundred percent should it turn out to be dangerous."

Xev takes the gun and examines it, seemingly impressed with its decoration of etched lines.

The last thing I wanted to do was to make this bastard feel good about himself. His juvo-mangled, gone-to-seed act might just be that, an act, but Xev is a survivor. He knows his best chance to get out of this mess is to stick with me. And if he's somehow involved? Giving him a gun might be the best way to find out.

"Drex is right. Why does he get the gun?" Klund says coming up to me. "He is a frigging thief and a drunk."

"If it comes to that," Hewlis growls, his large frame filling my vision, "I also know my way around a gun. You point and pull the trigger, right? You think I can't be trusted to do that?"

"I agree," Velez says. "He's not up to the job. Give the gun to me." Her eyes show the flash of mania, the twitch in her neck thrumming like the string on a guitar.

I push the chef away with the flat of my hand. She shouts out like I've punched her in the face. An over-reaction. Hewlis and Klund crowd me, followed by a vocal Rooba who seems to have lost her normal, implacable cool.

I get what's happening. Even though Hewlis and the rest can't sense *Ariadne's* empathic mind, it is still affecting them. Pushing them to the edge. The survivors are showing the symptoms of being close to such a strong and negative empathy field. It's only a matter of time before they all go mad. Luckily, time is what we don't have. I don't need no wafer countdown to tell me that.

I raise my gun and fire at the ceiling. It makes a reverberating boom in the small chamber. Velez drops to the floor with Klund, while Hewlis raises his hands.

"Calm down," I growl at them. "Bickering with me will get you nowhere. I'm making Xev my deputy, and that's final. No one else. And if you have a problem with that, know this: he's a murderer. A good one. And he enjoys it." I turn to Xev. "If any one of them steps out of line, shoot-to-kill. Understand?"

Velez is incensed. "The man is just an aide and well past it!"

"This ain't a democracy," I say. "Or have you forgotten I'm in charge? Now can it."

There are more noises of protest, but I'm not in the mood to listen.

"Where the hell is Boyd?" Drex says from somewhere behind me. "He's gone!"

neo-dawn

I PUSH everyone angrily away. Drex is right. Boyd has disappeared. I stare back down the corridor leading to this chamber. There are many turn-offs, other exits and no sign of the kid.

"What are you waiting for?" Hewlis says aggressively. "Aren't you going after him?"

I shake my head. "He's gone and you idiots gave him the opportunity to escape."

The engineer's face is still reddened and full of irrational anger. "You mean he could be the goddamn imposter?"

"No way!" Drex shouts. "It's not Boyd. I know him better than anybody. He's upset, that's all."

"About what?" I ask.

Drex shrugs. "About what's happened on this ship. It's hit him hard. Harder than you realise."

"So, he's the sensitive type, huh? Sensitive enough to run off on his own when staying with everyone here is the most sensible solution? Unless he's got something to hide that is."

Drex says nothing.

"Boyd could be in cahoots with that thing Pirella saw following us," Klund says.

Drex runs a stressed hand over his face. "He'll be back. I know him. He probably needs some time alone to get his head together."

"Time is something we don't have," I reply. "Do you know where he might've gone?"

"Boyd liked to hang out in Hydroponics, the lowest deck," Drex answers. "In the viewing portals. Plastiglass bubbles like the curved window of the Hospitality Suite, and large enough for a person to sit inside unnoticed."

"Then we should go find him," Hewlis says, visibly trying to calm himself.

I shake my head with irritation. "No. First I want to go and check on Glaxtinian's cabin. We'll visit Hydroponics afterwards. And when we find Boyd, he'll have some explaining to do."

I hold up my gun. "Anyone of you who ignores me again, won't live to regret it okay? Final warning."

The gun has a sobering effect on everyone. I guess that any one of them would be keen to get their hands on it. Or on the gun I gave to Xev.

We make our way to Glaxtinian's cabin. Drex leads everybody in tight formation with me and Xev taking up the rear.

I become aware of Pirella and Velez hissing at one another in a whispered argument. Pirella tries to step forward, but she is held back by the chef.

"I should never have trusted you!" Pirella spits, her thin arms flailing at the chef. "We wouldn't be in this goddamn mess and… Denny wouldn't be dead."

"I've told you to keep your mouth shut!" Velez replies, easily sweeping aside the younger girl.

"It was you who got inside Denny's head," Pirella continues. "You who made him—"

Velez punches Pirella in the face and she crumbles to the corridor floor as a jumble of arms and legs. Velez raises her fist again but stops in mid-motion when Xev violently jabs his gun into her neck.

"Don't you dare say anything!" the chef warns Pirella.

"If Velez tries to move, shoot her," I say coldly.

Xev twists the barrel of the gun and smiles. "Will do, boss."

I pull the sobbing girl to her feet. "What in space is going on between you two?" I ask her, realising I've been remiss in not investigating their relationship further. I blame the sudden appearance of the body-blank in Hospitality and my constant battle with *Ariadne*. Something was going on between them. Something involving Pirella's dead boyfriend, Denny. Was it a petty domestic dispute or something more sinister?

"She knows," Pirella says, pointing at Velez.

Xev swaps a glance with me. "Knows what?"

Pirella's eyes are adamant and sparkle from behind a barrage of tears. "She's… she's *Neo-Dawn!*"

"She's what?" Hewlis says to a shocked-looking Velez. "The terrorist gang that has been causing the Company trouble these last few months?"

I also know the name. Strategist Stranng warned me about them before I arrived upon the *Ariadne*. Neo-Dawn was responsible for the deaths of some important Company VIPs and other crimes.

"Of course not," Velez replies. "Look at me. I'm a chef. Not a fucking terrorist. The girl is just jealous."

Rooba appears at my shoulder. "Jealous of what, honey?"

"Her boyfriend Denny doubled up… if you know what I mean?" The chef replies with a leer. "Sometimes men want a real woman." She turns her attention to Pirella. "Not a mewling child."

"That's not true!" Pirella screams, lurching towards the chef. I easily hold her back.

Velez looks smug. "I think you know it is."

"Denny wouldn't. He just wouldn't!" Pirella shouts.

"He's a man," the chef replies with a sneer. "And he was my lover long before he met you."

"No!"

"If you're going to play adult games," Velez says, "you need to grow up."

"Tell me everything," I say to Pirella, focusing her attention away from the chef. "Tell me about Denny, how you met. Tell me about Velez and Neo-Dawn."

Pirella wipes her eyes. "I met Denny about two months ago at one of Daddy's functions," she says, the words spilling from her in a torrent. "A handsome waiter who couldn't stop looking at me. We fell in love. That's when I found out what he stood for. Against the Company and their tyranny. He told me about Velez, and others like her, who were resisting. I wasn't sure about it at first, but Denny explained to me what the Company was doing. Showed me stuff. Horrific things. And soon, I too, wanted to make a difference."

I hear Xev chuckle.

"Why's he laughing?" Pirella asks.

"Ignore him. What happened next?"

"I began to question everything in my life. To argue with Daddy's friends. Questioning them. But Denny said that wasn't enough. That I was talking to the wrong people. That's when he convinced me to come aboard this ship. He said that someone from a family as important as mine, making a protest in front of all those Company VIPs, would make a real difference."

I take in the information with no reaction, but it sounds to me like the girl was specifically targeted. "What kind of protest?"

"Once everyone had arrived at the party, I was to give a speech from Neo-Dawn, telling them who I was and why I was there—about what the Company is doing. How they run things. The deaths. The lies they tell about the Colony Worlds. The genetic experimentation. Everything."

"You traitorous little bitch!" Velez shouts.

I nod to Xev who pistol-whips the chef, giving her a bloodied lip.

"And I take it this speech was being recorded?"

Pirella nods. "Denny was going to broadcast what I was saying down to the planet, live on the dark-streams. To let people know there was resistance to the Company."

"Just a protest?" I'm confused. From what Stranng told me about Neo-Dawn, a passive protest doesn't sound right.

Pirella points at Velez. "It was her plan. I didn't like her, but Danny convinced me it was the right thing to do."

"You didn't suspect Denny might've been lying to you?"

Pirella's face hardens. "No! Why would he do that? He loved me. Despite what Velez says."

I turn to face the chef. "That's not the full story, is it?" I bark.

Velez licks at the line of blood pooling on her cut lip. "What the girl is saying is true. Apart from one thing… I'm not Neo-Dawn. Neither was Denny. We just spun her that story to get her to do what we wanted. Like I said, he was my lover. We hatched the plan together."

"No," Pirella whispers.

Klund takes an involuntary step backwards from the chef, like he's moving away from an unpleasant smell.

"If you're not Neo-Dawn, what reason could you have to do such a thing?" I ask.

"That's simple," Velez replies. "Revenge. Your wafer told you that I was demoted, but it didn't tell you why. It was that dried up old hag, Glaxtinian. She made a fool of me at one of her fancy VIP parties. She was drunk. No doubt on the same brand of brandy that your friend Xev pilfered from her cabin. Glaxtinian called me out of the galley and rebuked me in front of everyone. Said I was overrated. Said a lot of bad things. But I'm no walkover and gave as good as I got. The jumped-up cow didn't like 'staff' talking back to her and used her influence in the Company to punish and demote me."

"Glaxtinian?" I say. "Did you have anything to do

with her death? Or the gassing of the ship?"

Velez shakes her head. "I wish I'd been the one to shoot the bitch in the gut. Hell, I might've even done it if I'd had the chance. But… *it wasn't me*. The plan was to shame her and all the VIPs on a live stream. To bring her down a peg or two. To give her a dose of her own medicine. The gassing changed all that. We were just as much victims as everyone else."

The chef's neck is twitching more than it has done before. It's a revelation, one that could end her career and her life. I wish I could read her, but *Ariadne* is broadcasting too loudly on the empathic spectrum for me to judge the truth of her words. But empathy isn't my only skill. "That's not all, is it?"

"You don't think fooling one of their own to denounce Glaxtinian and the rest of the Company VIP cronies, would've been a sweet revenge for what she did to me?" Velez says with incredulity.

"Was that the full plan, Pirella?" I ask the still sobbing girl, whose delicate fingers are wrapped around her amber necklace.

She nods.

"What kind of half-assed idea is that?" Xev says with incredulity. "You risked everything to get this girl aboard only to give a damn speech? Then what? Once the Company realised what she did, she'd be arrested and interrogated. You saw how easily she broke down just now. She would've given you up in a heartbeat. Both of you."

"As long as Glaxtinian went down with me, I wouldn't give a damn!" Velez replies.

I believe her. I can't sense her resentment, but it's

plastered all over her face.

"But that wasn't the plan," Velez continues. "Me and Denny made arrangements to be a long way away when that happened. We were gonna leave the Company and set up a whole new life with one of its rivals."

"The Company does hate to be shamed," Hewlis says, nodding. "If Velez and Denny managed to broadcast such a speech, careers would be ended— over and done with."

I agree with the engineer, but it doesn't feel right. "Xev hit it on the head. *That's a hell of a lot of trouble to go to for just a shaming.*"

"Simple payback," Velez says, a pleased sneer crossing her face. "With a patsy in place to take all the blame. Denny targeted Pirella specifically."

"No!" Pirella shouts. "No way."

I place a calming hand on the girl's shoulder.

"We were after someone like her for a while," Velez says, the hate in her voice rising. "A rich brat. A son or daughter of a VIP with enough Company clout to aid our cause. Pirella Qelline was the third and easiest target Denny tried his little act on. And she fell for it, like the stupid, stuck-up little rich girl she is."

The girl shakes her head vehemently. "Denny loved me."

Pirella is distraught. And, I believe, no liar. It seems very clear to me that she was duped by Denny and Velez. "You should've told me this earlier."

"Velez threatened to kill me if I didn't keep quiet."

"The Skilled always get to the bottom of things, sooner or later. Or don't you remember me telling you that?"

"Now what?" Velez says bullishly. "You know how we fooled the girl, what we were up to. But we never got the chance to go through with it. You're just wasting time. Time we don't have."

"Well this is a turn-up," says Xev. "Vatic has captured a fucking terrorist cell. And who's his goddamn right-hand man? It's that good, old, reliable bastard, Xev Tranth. Shit, I might just get my damn career back." He screws his gun into Velez's cheek, making her wince.

"I told you, we are not Neo-Dawn," she says. "That was just a line to spin to the girl. And we did nothing. You haven't got anything on us."

"When Vatic gets us out of this mess, the Company will be looking for someone to blame," Xev says with more than a little glee. "You think they are not gonna dump on you from high? Neo-Dawn or not? You're done and fucked, Velez. Conspiracy to act against the Company. And witnessed. You want me to kill her now?"

I allow his question to hang in the air for a few seconds, but if I wanted the chef to sweat, she isn't obliging.

"No, but keep an eye on her," I say finally.

esta

WE MAKE our way towards Glaxtinian's cabin. The revelation of Velez's plan hanging in the air like a sickly shroud. And yet, I'm sure I'm missing something. Velez was going to a lot of trouble just to name and shame Glaxtinian.

Rooba walks with Pirella, one long, slim, red arm draped around her trembling shoulders. Klund lopes next to them, seemingly lost in his own thoughts while Drex and Hewlis lead the way.

Xev drops back to talk to me again, keeping his gun trained on Velez and the rest of the troupe. "Thanks for the vote of support," he says with his mangled smile. "We make a good team."

"This chummy act of yours is really starting to grate," I whisper, my voice a low growl.

"Hey! That's no way to talk to your partner."

"Partner? Don't make me laugh."

"You don't trust me?" he says, waving the gun. "Then why give me this? Maybe I shot Glaxtinian in the fucking gut?"

"You didn't."

"How can you know that?"

"For starters, you've not shot me. The person or persons behind what's going on here wouldn't waste a second in eliminating me. I'm the biggest threat to them. To what's going down here."

"Maybe I'm playing a waiting game? I'm still a clever fucker, despite appearances."

"Cut the crap, Xev. I don't know what happened to you since the war, but you ain't the Xev I left behind. You're a mess. Washed up. I don't need no empathy to tell me that."

The smile stretching at the tight, ruined skin of Xev's face fades to be replaced with a twist of anger. "I survived, but no thanks to you. When I needed your help, where the hell were you? I sent you message after fucking message but got nothing back."

"You asked *me* for help?" I'm shocked. I'm the last person I'd expect him to contact. I'm a Skilled and Xev hated all of us.

"I told you… I was on the wrong side of the coup and desperate. I needed all the fucking help I could get."

"You obviously made it, or you wouldn't be here."

"With no help from you. That came from *elsewhere*. You didn't receive *any* of my communications?"

A quick shake of my head. "After the war, and especially after the coup, I wasn't interested in the Company… or in anything for that matter. I found the slowest colony ship and put myself aboard and into hibernation."

"You did what?" Xev splutters. "I thought you looked like you've just come out of a faulty hibernation pod. What in fuck did you do that for?"

"I was tired of taking sides. Weary. I just wanted to get away and do a bit of farming."

"Vatic? A farmer? I've never heard anything so fucking ridiculous. You were a goddamn war hero. An Honorary member of the Second Executive! All you had to do was keep your head down, toe the line and you were made for fucking life. Why would you throw that away?"

"What I did in the war…"

"You did what you had to do!" Xev spits. "We all did. Do or fucking die. There's no guilt in that. What makes you think you're so goddamn different?"

"I killed… *I killed millions.*"

Xev shrugs. "Like I said, you did what you had to do. And once you've killed one enemy soldier, what difference does a few more make? It was them or us. And we won, thanks to unfeeling bastards like yourself."

"A *few* more? I'm a monster. And you know it."

"What the hell has happened to you? It's not like Vatic to come over all emotional. And you sure were one unfeeling prick."

"It's you I'm wondering about," I reply. "I thought you hated me and all the Skilled. What changed?"

"That's simple. I have one to thank for my freedom."

"A Skilled came to *your* rescue?"

"Sure. I wasn't a fan of your breed. You were cold but by space you were effective. And you're surprisingly honourable under all that arrogance. It was a favour repaid."

"That's quite some favour. What did you do, save their life?"

"Don't play dumb, Vatic. You know who it was. Your old partner, Esta."

The mention of that name sends cold slivers of ice through me. I feel a sudden anger, a rage almost. "What? I'll never forget that you ordered me to kill her!"

Xev's mangled face twists into an expression of confusion. "But you didn't kill her, did you? If you had, I wouldn't be here. It was Esta who got me off. Her debt repaid."

I can hear Xev's words, but they are not properly penetrating my brain. "What?"

"The war was ending," Xev says. "Don't you remember? Esta was a valuable double agent. Your partner. And then came the orders to terminate her. You didn't want to do it. Hell, I didn't want to either. It was a political decision and a bad one. She'd been a great asset and still was. So, I warned her. Let her know what the Company was up to. When you came back after your last mission together and told me she was dead, I didn't ask any questions. I assumed you were spinning me a line. You Skilled were always thick with one another."

"No," I state adamantly. "I shot her. I will never forget it. *I can't forget it.*"

"Then how am I here? How am I alive? Not due to any help from you that's for sure. I was scheduled for a fucking execution. Me! Xev Tranth! After everything I did for the Company in the war. I was incensed, angry and, I'll admit it. I was afraid. On the morning

I was due to be unceremoniously dumped out of the nearest airlock, I received a last-minute reprieve. Afterwards, came a four-word message."

We are now even.

"It was signed *E*."

"No! I watched Esta die!" I shout, stumbling and coming to rest against the corridor wall. "There was no way she survived."

Xev waves everyone to stop, bringing his head next to mine, while keeping the buzz-gun pointed at the entourage and particularly at Velez. Hewlis gives me a concerned look, while the chef sneers. The other faces are just blurs.

"I've replayed her death again and again in my mind," I whisper, my voice a thin croak. "I shot her."

Xev shakes his head. "There can be no doubt that she's alive. All those who ordered her death have since been killed—and not in good ways. Those guys suffered, you know what I mean? Revenge, plain and simple. It had to be Esta. She hated betrayal more than anything. She was taking the biggest risks of us all, working for both sides. And the Company wanted to throw her away like so much fucking trash."

"No," I croak. "No."

The news shocks me, rattling through me to my core and I momentarily lose myself, unconsciously forgetting to hold back *Ariadne*. Her terrible thoughts screech into me and I crumple. Part of me wants to let the ship's entity devour me, to swallow me whole, but my sense of self-preservation takes over and I force

Ariadne away again. As I push against her invasive mind, new memories are freed from deep inside me, memories that are at odds with what I know to be true. Opposing recollections commingling and fighting one other for precedence. Fragmented recollections colliding and breaking like the shards of glass in the smashed hotel mirror that has haunted me ever since I came out of hypersleep. And instead of my own, guilty accusing eyes staring back at me, I see the flashing, golden eyes of Esta...

I take a deep breath of the heavy, ozone smelling air. The Wormer has its own atmosphere—a thin envelope allowing me to breathe and to observe an amazing starscape, although most of it is hidden by the cloud of dust these machines spew out—hanging in space like a polluted, stained comet.

The Milky Way, half-obscured, extends up and over my head, surrounded by a myriad of pinprick stars. Andromeda is beautiful set against such stark blackness. An astounding vista, but cold. I feel myself shivering.

"Vatic?"

The voice is faraway, faint. A woman's voice. The timbre is familiar, painful. I can't answer, I mustn't answer.

"Vatic! Come inside. And close those damn doors, it's freezing."

I turn and stare back into what I recognise as a bedroom. I've seen this vista before, hundreds of times. A double bed sits against the far wall, a black satin over-sheet thrown onto the worn carpet, the bedclothes crumpled. I leave the balcony with its spectacular views, walk inside and close the doors, recognising fitments that seemed to have been seared into my brain: twin bedside lights each with an orange lampshade standing atop cupboards with chrome handles. A cabinet stacked with booze and littered with half-empty cocktail glasses. A large black and white print of a reclining woman smoking a stylised cigarette—her bright red lips the only colour. A crumpled blue dress lying on the floor next to an upturned, sling back shoe. A dressing table above which hangs a mirror with my reflection. I'm wearing a black suit with an open-collared white shirt. Underneath, I glimpse the grey of a skinsuit. I'm muscular, taut—and dangerous. And those eyes… they sparkle and burn like twin, blue, angry suns. Bright and steely—manic with the fervour of truth and deserving retribution.

"Vatic," the voice continues. "Fix me a drink while I'm getting ready."

I then notice the buzz-gun in my hand. Palm-coded, deadly.

"Vatic? Are you deaf?"

A naked woman enters the room from the en suite. Red hair flows from her head in a cascade of curls. Golden eyes stab out of her face. Eyes like my own. Haunted, wired, unnatural in colour. She's a Skilled. "What the hell is this?" she says calmly, her finely chiselled chin dipping towards the buzz-gun.

And then I speak those words. The words I dread to hear: "I know it's you." My voice is cold, empty.

"Vatic, let me explain. Let me—"

But I don't let her explain. Instead, I press the stud and shoot. A single shot. She crumples over, landing on the dressing table with a crash, the mirror smashing everywhere.

I watch her die, the blood seeping from the hole in her side as big as a melon, my cold, blue eyes glittering back at me from so many broken shards.

"Oh, Vatic…" she gasps.

…The scene as it has played out a thousand times in my mind. The horror and the guilt branded into my subconscious. Those myriad accusing eyes. My eyes. And yet this time, the memory has a transparent quality.

Unreal. Like I'm seeing it from far away.

The figures move and speak like ghosts. Ghosts that fade and disappear. I see myself lying on the same hotel room floor. Esta squatting above me. Attaching something to my head. And it all comes crashing back.

I was brain-squeezed… Esta forced me to believe I'd killed her!

Since I've been recovering from my near-death in hibernation, my memories have been a jumble. But it wasn't the hibernation that scrambled my brain. It was something more sinister. The effort of keeping *Ariadne* away from my mind has somehow weakened the hold of these implanted memories.

"Vatic," Xev says with concern. "You okay?"

I come back to myself. "She brain-squeezed me," I gasp, feeling an incredible sense of relief.

"Esta? But why? Why on earth would she need to

do that?"

"I had my orders," I spit angrily.

"You mean you were really going to go through with it, you were really going to kill her?"

I nod, the memories slowly falling back into place. "She planted terrible memories of grief deep into my mind. She wanted me to suffer for her death—*a death that never happened*. Her revenge, I guess. I'd gone there to kill her. Like the mindless Company drone who had killed all those millions in the war."

"I never thought you'd go through with it," Xev whispers. "Why?"

"That was me back then, wasn't it? *The man of Black and Blue and White.*"

"But why didn't Esta kill you? She knew you were coming for her. I warned her."

"It's simple," I reply, coming back to myself. "She didn't want me dead, she wanted me alive and suffering."

Xev gives me a confused look.

"She loved me." Three simple words, words that have hounded me ever since. Cutting into me. Burning me with hot knives of guilt.

"A Skilled in love? No way. You are heartless bastards and Esta was a hard-faced fucker. Hell, you were a good match."

"She knocked me out and used a memory-squeeze to change the version of events. Why else plant such feelings of grief and remorse inside of me? She wanted me to know exactly how the betrayal of her love hurt her. *She wanted me to feel that forever.* That was the hook that kept everything else in place. The one truth that held the rest of the lie together. *Her love for me.*"

Xev stares into my one good eye, the words registering across his face. His uneven eyebrows furrowing, before letting out a low laugh. "Wow! A Skilled in love. I would never have believed it. No wonder you tried to hide yourself in the Colonies. Why you wanted to become a fucking farmer. Esta is one cruel bitch."

"You were right. Me, a farmer? It's a ridiculous notion. But I couldn't see through it. I couldn't see past my own guilt and grief."

Xev chuckles.

"What?"

"All this time I thought you were the best Skilled I'd ever known. Hell, I even admired you, not that I'd have told you that. But Vatic out-smarted by someone else? *By Esta?* …I would've never imagined that in a hundred fucking lifetimes. Esta played you for a fool, Vatic. She duped you. A farmer in the Colonies?" he repeats with incredulity. "I can't quite fucking believe it." His chuckles turn into full-on laughter.

I pull myself up to stand on shaking legs, aware of everyone looking at me. "The show's over!" I shout at them. "Get a move on!"

There is a lot to process, and it will take time, time that I don't have. And even though my mind is still adjusting, there is a new feeling. *Excitement.*

Esta is alive.

I vow to get off this ship and go and find her.

glaxtinian

"GET GOING!" I say, ignoring the confused expressions, although the sneer on Eric Klund's face sticks out like a sore thumb. A thumb that needs to be slapped sometime soon if he doesn't change his attitude.

Xev gives me a sideways glance. And even through the folds of his face, I can see that he thinks I'm diminished. I'm no longer the Vatic he thinks I was.

Fuck him.

I walk past everyone to the front, instructing Xev to bring up the rear, my thoughts still jumbled.

After a few silent minutes where I can feel everyone's eyes burning into my back, Rooba Jen comes up to me, walking on my shoulder like an official consort. The Jen are single-minded and power-orientated. I'm in charge—a bright, white flame she finds impossible to ignore. Forget that the ship is gonna get blown apart sometime soon, that I just suffered some peculiar mental breakdown, and that I'm an emaciated stick with one manic eye—I'm the top dog and that's all that matters.

She says nothing, content to glide along at my side, her head tilted in my direction, as if listening to my thoughts.

"Don't stand so goddamn close."

Rooba dutifully takes a step back. But I know her obedience is only feigned.

To me, she's just another suspect. "Don't play your games," I spit in her direction. "It won't work."

The Jen seems pleased I'm speaking to her, regardless of my tone.

"Not even when you know I'm willing to become whoever you want me to be?" she whispers. "To take on any physical shape, face, or gender to satisfy your needs... *even then?*"

The face of Esta flicks unwelcome into my mind. Her large, wired golden eyes and red, crazy hair. I subconsciously ready myself for the wave of grief and guilt that always accompanies her name. This time it doesn't come. I'm lost for a moment until I realise the new truth. *Esta is still alive.*

I shake my head. "I don't need anyone, especially not a copy."

"A copy? So, you do have someone in mind?"

"Don't mess with me," I reply, annoyed at my slip. "You're a suspect like anyone else. An augmented individual such as yourself, with your stripped-down DNA, would be easy to mimic. That puts you at the top of my suspect list, especially as you're not on the official ship's roster."

Rooba shrugs, her array of clearly visible breasts quivering under the chiffon of her sheer robes. "You must know that all Jen are copyrighted and recorded?

Each genetic strand stamped by the Company? They may own the genetic processes, but I paid for them. In sweat, blood and everything else you can imagine. I'm most definitely not an imposter. I never understand why everyone else is so desperate to hang onto their original genetic identity. DNA is unimportant, or do the Skilled think otherwise?"

I don't answer her question. I was created in a damn test-tube. Space knows what my genome looks like under a microscope. I've never had the inclination to check myself out. I can't imagine it's anything pretty. The bottom line—I don't own my DNA either.

We arrive at Glaxtinian's cabin a short while later. The hatch is closed, but the lock isn't engaged, probably left that way by Xev, but I'm taking no chances. I kick it open revealing a reasonably large, but functional room. I usher everyone inside and get Xev to guard the door. I don't want anyone else running off.

Glaxtinian clearly didn't have time to unpack. Her cases are neatly stacked in one corner, apart from the ones broken into by Xev. A bottle of brandy, half empty, lies on her bed. I'm surprised to find an en-suite head and shower unit. This is the kind of accommodation reserved for the Strategist or another high-ranking member of the crew. But then again, Glaxtinian was a Company Grandee, and *an Arbiter*—they expect the best. She was here to stay… that's a fact.

Could she have been killed by the person who's cabin she took? I consider the possibility longer than it merits, before discounting it out of hand. But Glaxtinian's presence on this ship could've put someone's nose out of joint… and that someone was most likely Professor Chandrasekhar.

Glaxtinian's job was that of ball-breaker. And after what Xev told me about the professor, I guess he's the type to try and keep his balls intact. Shooting Glaxtinian in the gut in front of the entire crew doesn't sound like the move of a survivor. The professor might be responsible, but it seems too clumsy for someone who's survived this long at the top of his game. I guess he's lying dead somewhere on this ship. Gassed, like almost everyone else.

I go over to the room's single desk that doubles as a dressing table. A few typical items, recently unpacked, lie on top. A brush, make-up sticks, tissues. There's also a winking data-centre. Her personal device. Locked and bio-linked to Glaxtinian with no way inside.

Instead, I systematically search the drawers, not expecting to find anything, and discover a simple folder. One word is printed on the cover: *Ariadne*.

The Company is paranoid. The days of hacking, of illegal access to wafers and data-centres are long-gone. But they still fear the possibility of an enemy agent somehow breaking their incredible encryption systems. Perhaps it's because they're working on doing the same to their rivals. The practical result? The Company has gone back to using good, old-fashioned paper.

I open the folder, expecting an alarm to go off, but nothing. Inside is a sheaf of documents.

Ariadne design specs.

And pages and pages of printed notes from

Glaxtinian. Mostly to do with costings and targets. My hunch about why she was aboard was correct.

"What have you found?" Hewlis says.

"Looks like Glaxtinian—and the Company— were not happy with how Professor Chandrasekhar was running things. From what I can tell, she came aboard with the intention of taking control of the project. Is that possible Klund?" I ask the geek. "Was the professor being side-lined?"

"The professor's work upon *Ariadne,* was ground-breaking and quite, quite brilliant. I cannot imagine that the Company would want to replace him. It makes no sense to me. The man is a first-order genius."

"But didn't you say *Ariadne* had gone insane? That doesn't sound like brilliance to me, it stinks of failure."

Klund shakes his head as if I've said the most stupid thing. "*Ariadne* was a prototype. Prototypes have their teething problems. The first step in a larger program. Breakthroughs do not happen overnight. It takes years and years of work, refining and adjusting."

"What's happened aboard this ship is more than a goddamn teething problem. And it seems the Company got wind all was not well." I hold up the folder. "Chandrasekhar's days were numbered. The ship's schematics have been augmented without Company approval. There's also a series of logged incidents detailing some of the problems aboard. And rumours and gossip concerning the professor and his fractious relationship with the crew—particularly the Strategist who he was at odds with. Which means..."

"Glaxtinian must've had a spy aboard," Xev finishes for me.

"The Company wouldn't exist without lies and intrigue," Velez says dismissively. "I've not met one grandee who didn't get where they were without bending the truth, without manipulation or simple threat."

I can't disagree with the chef, although I'm guessing her ire comes from her demotion. VIP chefs get to the top of their profession by merit alone. No amount of lying, extortion or skulduggery would make an iota of difference to the quality of food she was able to produce.

Pirella's eyes flick towards Velez as she speaks—a frightened dog reacting to an overbearing master. The chef sure played Pirella for a fool.

I continue my search, rummaging through Glaxtinian's luggage, but find nothing of interest. Just clothes, and expensive ones at that. I'm about to give up when I feel something in a zipped compartment. I open it and pull out an antique, silver-rimmed photo-frame. Inside is a digivid of Mandibald Glaxtinian with her arm around a very attractive woman. Standing in front of them both is a blonde boy in his early teens. Unmistakably, Murton Boyd.

boyd

"BOYD? I don't get it," Hewlis says, taking the digivid off me and staring at it.

The screen changes to show other photos. The same three people. Boyd as a baby. Boyd as a toddler, Boyd growing up.

I expel an annoyed breath. This investigation is one tangled mess. Nothing is coming together. Nothing fits with one another. Glaxtinian is at the centre of all these events, though, that much is for sure. Her death was the catalyst that somehow caused this on-board horror show. And at the back of everything? *Ariadne.* Chiding away at me. Trying to force her way back into my mind, hampering my investigation.

"He is related to that woman?" Klund says.

"Seems that way," I reply, annoyed with myself. I should've paid more attention to Boyd from the start. The kid was upset about something, that was for sure. I thought it was simply everybody dying, but it was one person that Boyd was grieving for. *Mandibald Glaxtinian.*

I round on Drex, roughly pushing the kid back

against the cabin wall. "What the hell do you know about this?"

"It's not for me to say," he replies bullishly.

I consider pistol-whipping him some more but decide on a different approach. I've already beat up on this kid. And despite everything, he's still just that. *A kid.* "Look, Drex," I begin softly. "You need to tell me. Out with it."

"Boyd swore me to secrecy. I can't—"

"Did he also make you swear to keep quiet when yours and other's lives may depend on it?" I snap at him.

Drex shakes his head, his thick, greasy hair sticking to the sweat of his face. "Glaxtinian… she was Boyd's mother."

"His goddamn mother!" Hewlis exclaims.

Drex nods and swallows. "Yeah."

"Then why are you a sublieutenant and not him?" I ask. "Hell, why is he even a corpsman at all? With her influence, he could start out as a goddamn officer."

Drex's voice is calm and measured, but his bottom lip trembles. "They didn't get on. Not for a long time. Glaxtinian left when he was just a kid. Soon after, his other mother died. Boyd blamed Glaxtinian for that."

"Boyd killed Glaxtinian?" Velez says, her arched eyebrows furrowing. "You think it was him who shot her in the gut with a buzz-gun for revenge? …Maybe I misjudged the kid."

Drex gives an emphatic shake of his head, his eyes still on me. "He's not been out of my sight all day. Glaxtinian didn't show up at the party and I think Boyd was hoping she never came aboard. That she wasn't gassed with the others. That's why I was resistant to go search the ship as you ordered. I knew Boyd would be freaked."

"You should've told me. Maybe Boyd knows something about what's going on here."

"I doubt it. He was as shocked as I was when he learned of his mother's death, that she'd been murdered. You all saw that. Deep down, I think he knew she was dead with everyone else. That's probably why he ran off."

"Unless you were in on it too," I say. "You seemed very close."

"I've known Boyd for a long time. But that's not what happened. Things have changed between him and Glaxtinian recently. They've been in contact with one another."

"He knew she was coming aboard? Coming to stay?"

Drex nods. "There's more."

"Boyd was her secret agent aboard the *Ariadne,* am I right?"

"Yeah, I think so. Although he was tight-lipped about it. He had codes to get into some of the off-limit areas."

"He had what?" Klund exclaims.

I wave away the geek's outburst with an irritated sweep of my hand. "That makes sense," I say to Drex. "Glaxtinian was an Arbiter. And we can assume she was sent here to take over the project from Chandrasekhar. Or at least get in his way."

"It wasn't like that," Drex protests. "Boyd wasn't given any direct orders from her, Glaxtinian just wanted him to sniff around. At first, he wasn't interested in helping her. 'Told her to go stick it' is how Boyd put it to me. But she was his mum and I think that's what changed his mind."

"Is that everything?" I say, allowing the anger I'm feeling to deliberately sink into my voice. "Because if I find you're lying to me again, it'll be you who's next to get a buzz-gun in the gut. You get me?"

Drex drops his head. "Yeah."

Hewlis twists his massive bulk to stare at him. "Why didn't you say something before?"

The kid's voice is an empty rasp. "Like I said. He's my mate and mates stick together."

Every time I find out something about what went down here on the *Ariadne*, it turns up as a dead end. Still, maybe Boyd will have more to say when we find him. He could've spun any line to Drex, but I admit it—I've nothing to go on.

I turn to face everyone else. "We are all going to die unless we can stop *Ariadne*. That means that I need to know everything. I don't care about who you are or what you've done. If anyone else is hiding something, I want to know what it is. It could mean the difference between life and death."

hydroponics

I CHECK the time.

23:11

Fifty or so minutes until Stranng gets his wish of blowing me and the other survivors out of hyperspace. I bet he can't wait.

But I'm Vatic. I cannot fail!

I see a vision of Esta sitting astride me, attaching the brain-squeezer to my head.

Is this the mission where the odds finally overtake me?

I catch my thoughts. What the hell did Esta do to me?

I bring up the ship schematics on my wafer. The bottom deck has a series of viewing ports, allowing crew members to view the cosmos at close hand—like Drex mentioned. It's as far away from a Company ship as to be ridiculous. Chandrasekhar had style—probably one of the reasons the Company wanted him controlled. They are not fond of ostentation, although I understand the professor's motivation.

The ship is a showcase. A warship is designed to blow other ships out of space and into the afterlife. Not a high-end VIP cruise-liner. It certainly wouldn't have a goddamn hospitality suite, nor would it have an enormous hydroponics deck complete with viewing ports. But show works. Gets the punters to sit up and take notice and pay their money.

The Company I remember wouldn't be impressed. Still, I must give the professor his dues. The guy was pushing two-hundred. To survive this long in the Company means he must've known what he was doing. Until *Ariadne* changed all that.

"Drex … lead the way to the bottom deck."

Drex complies, a tense look prematurely aging his youthful features. Boyd disappearing has hit him hard. I don't like the kid. He's the pushy, belligerent type that will barge his way to the top, but I believe he's genuinely worried for his friend.

Is he the imposter?

I can't quite see it. The phony—whoever it is—is playing a clever game. Sure, the body-blank being found was a misstep, but they could've been planning this for months. Plenty of time to get a full back-story on their victims and associates.

We make a quick exit from the cabin and head down the staircase to the bottom of the ship and Hydroponics.

Drex leads us around a corner and I trip over an enormous door bolt lying on the floor, my thoughts diverted to what remains of the hydroponics hatch. It's been ripped off its hinges. Drex was right, it appears that something managed to get out, rather than breaking in.

"Hewlis, with me," I bark, and the engineer arrives at my side.

"What the—?" he mutters.

"What the hell could've done this?" I finish for him. "That's what I'm asking you."

Hewlis shakes his shaggy head. "Something very strong."

"A cargo exo, maybe?"

Hewlis shakes his head again. "The stairwell is too small to get something that large in here."

"Then what did it? What broke out?"

He shrugs. "Like I said... something, very, very strong."

His words cause a few nervous glances from the already agitated troop. My eyes dart at Drex. "You think Boyd is somewhere in Hydroponics?"

Drex shrugs. "I hope so. Like I said, he used to come here a lot. To hide in the viewing ports."

"Well let's go find him."

We step through the broken door and onto a metal walkway suspended half-way between ceiling and floor. I'm hit by a sea of green and the sickly smell of vegetation and decomposition. Hydroponics sections are usually warmer than the other parts of the ship, but something has gone dreadfully wrong down here. Despite being on the outer hull, the heat is oppressive. I feel sweat collecting along my hairline, under my chin and down the back of my neck.

The place is stuffed with plants and small trees fed by curling hydroponic pipes creating a forest-like feel. I remember Elbaz's domes back in the now destroyed

Zeta-Karst Labs and realise he was a true master. This is nothing on the scale of what he was able to achieve, but for a Company ship, it's unprecedented. From what I can see, the deck is twice as high as the others and stretches the width and length of the ship.

"It shouldn't be this hot down here," Klund says, examining the wilted greenery with alarm.

"He's not wrong," Hewlis whistles. "Still, this place is sure off the scale."

"You've not been down here before?" I ask him. "I thought engineers had access to every part of the ship?"

"I'm an engineer, not a hydroponics expert. A sub-light engine specialist. Which means I'm either stuck inside some thrust tube or monitoring essential systems." The engineer's lips twist into a sneer. "And besides, this place was off-limits to low-rankers like me."

"Unless their VIP parents gave them the access codes," Velez says, wincing as Xev pushes his gun into her spine.

"We should not have come down here," Klund says, looking agitated. "This place was designed especially by the professor. Only top bridge personnel have permission to enter."

"You mean he's responsible for this deck?" Xev says with a whistle. "Wow! I knew he was a grandee from the old school, but this is off the goddamn fucking scale."

"Have you also noticed that the gravity is a little less than one gee?" Drex says. "It's one of the reasons why Boyd used to sneak down here. It reminded him of home."

"Welcome to the Company," Velez spits, looking around her as if this was some obscene display. "Welcome to the world of *the haves* and the *have nots.*"

"Everyone in the Company has the chance to excel, to better themselves," Drex says, an agitated expression on his face.

"You don't really believe that? Do you, Sublieutenant?" Velez replies, her eyes roving over the trees and plants surrounding us on all sides. "How did you get aboard this damn flagship in the first place? By merit? By working harder than those around you? By being the best? Because that's how I got where I used to be, a rare exception to the Company rule. But you? You're here because you're the friend of Boyd who just happened to be connected to a Company high-flier."

Drex doesn't answer. I guess the chef's words are too close to the mark. I'm also an exception to the rule. Although in the case of the Skilled, we were helped by genetic augmentation.

"This place is amazing," Rooba says, ignoring the confrontation, her red, heavily lashed eyes flashing this way and that. "We had parks back on the colonies. If you can call them that. Fake grass and screens. I've never seen or smelled anything like it."

"You've never been inside a hydroponics bay?" Hewlis asks.

Rooba shakes her head. "Why would I?"

I notice the plants are wilting and sick-looking. Some of the stems and branches have been stripped bare of leaves. I wonder if it's just the heat that has affected them. "You think the gas came down as far as here?" I ask.

"We didn't find any bodies on this level," Drex says. "It's where we started our search. The place was deserted."

"It'll all be so much dust if we don't find a way of stopping the ship real soon," Velez says with an irritated shake of her head. "So what if Boyd killed his mother, that bitch Glaxtinian? Or was working for her? Or whatever? What the hell does it have to do with what's happened here? Even if we find him and he confesses everything, it's not going to stop the goddamn ship or pull it out of hyperspace."

"You really need to stop talking," Xev says. "Whatever happens, you're done for, sister. Dead and buried."

Velez shrugs, but she is making a valid point. However, I disagree with her. I'm convinced the murder of Glaxtinian is the key to solve this mystery. My gut speaking to me, my instinct. As to why I believe this? I have no idea.

I turn a right-angled corner on the walkway, and I'm met by the eerie lights of hyperspace flashing from a recessed portal below—like an amphitheatre. The scene would be beautiful and mesmerising except for one thing. Torn limbs discarded like the broken arms and legs of a dolly and the tell-tale splatter and splash of blood.

"No!" Drex shouts, racing forward.

Pirella screams, followed by the sounds of shock and disgust. Lying on the steps down to the viewing port is the decapitated head of Murton Boyd. His blue eyes staring back at us with a frozen look of terror on his face.

ripped

I EXAMINE what's left of Boyd's body while Xev takes up guard duty with his gun raised. My assessment is a simple one...

The kid has been ripped apart.

Arms and legs torn out of their sockets, his head, still trailing part of his oesophagus and other bits of flesh, pulled off his torso and thrown away. I've seen death many times, but even I'm shocked by this grisly horror show. The splash of fresh crimson blood against the green of this place is somehow obscene. I shudder.

Hewlis crouches down to examine Boyd's bloodied and ripped torso. "The mechanical force to do something like this would've been immense," he says.

"You're not squeamish?"

The engineer shakes his head. "Never have been. A body is just another machine, albeit beautiful and perfectly designed—it uses all the same physical principles."

I take in his words with a nod of my head. "What do you think did this?"

He stands up. "I dunno. It could be that exoskeleton you mentioned before, but it'd have to be souped-up. My question is why? Why not shoot him? Or just crush his throat or head. Why rip him apart?"

"Maybe it was personal?" Rooba says, the Jen's voice distant and far away.

"But who would want to do this to Boyd?" Drex says, unable to take his eyes off his friend's decapitated head. "He didn't have an enemy in the world."

"Didn't he?" I reply. "Boyd was working for Glaxtinian. Maybe he was killed because of his association with her? Especially if he was sneaking around the ship as her spy. But that's only speculation. What we need is hard evidence."

I check all parts of Boyd's body. Even the lumps of viscera and torn flesh.

Boyd's right fist is still clenched at the end of his discarded right arm. I pull apart the fingers not expecting to find anything. Two long silver hairs are trapped under Boyd's still-pink fingernails. Thick and greasy—Pirella's boy with silver hair and the face of an old man, perhaps?

I consider another possibility, one that has been bothering me for a while now… that there's something other than human aboard this ship. Some monster able to pull Boyd apart limb from limb and break its way through a hydraulic ship's door. If I could test the hairs for DNA, that would give me some answers. But it's not as if genome sequencers are a common feature of a warship. Sure, they're used at birth for ID purposes, or before, if the parents decide on augmenting their children. Outside the study of paediatrics, they are difficult to get a hold of. A typical warship wouldn't have such equipment aboard, but *Ariadne* is as about as far away from *typical* as you can get.

"Something is out there!" Klund says eerily, echoing my thoughts and breaking me out of my inner reverie. "The girl, Pirella saw it, so did your rude friend, Xev."

"Let's say you're right," I reply, rounding on him. "Who or what is it?"

Klund seems lost for words.

"We're all dead anyway," Velez says. "You've got no way of getting us out of this and you know it. Either this thing will kill us, or your friend out there in hyperspace will blow the ship apart."

"Can it, Velez!" I order.

The chef ignores me. "There must be another way off this ship. If *he* got aboard, then surely we can get off?" Velez says, nodding towards me. "He must've arrived in a ship. And what about the *Ariadne's* transports?"

"All destroyed when I crashed into the cargo bay." I reply.

"But there must be escape pods or something similar?"

"Sure there are," Hewlis replies to the agitated chef. "Located along the stern on the bridge deck. But they can't be used in hyperspace."

"There's escape pods?" Rooba says. "Then why can't Vatic pilot us out of here. Surely that's a better option? Better than certain death if we stay aboard."

The engineer shakes his mammoth head, his grey,

curly hair swinging against his temples. "They are single-person only. Reserved for the bridge crew. Fully automatic. You may launch yourself off the ship and, if the pods don't break up in the Snag Array field, you'll only have a very small chance of returning to normal space alive."

"Well I'm willing to take my chances," Velez says. "It's better odds than what we presently have. I'm getting sick to death of following you up and down this damn ship, waiting for the inevitable with your best friend sticking his gun in my back."

"There's no way you'd be able to get a pod out of hyperspace," I say. "That's suicide."

"Well it sounds like a better option."

"You know what, Velez" I say. "Maybe I should let you go, to take your chances against the void and against whatever monster did this to Boyd. You sure deserve it after what you were going to pull on Pirella, but you ain't going nowhere. No one is."

"Then at least give us something to protect ourselves with," the chef replies bullishly. "There must be an armoury on this ship?"

"You ain't getting a gun, sister," Xev says. "Now that *would be* suicide."

"But she's right."

I glance away from Xev to see Drex standing above the open viewing portal, his face lit from below by the flashing lights of hyperspace. "If you hadn't taken our guns, Boyd would've been able to defend himself. He'd be alive now."

"Whatever killed him," I say, "killed him because he ignored my orders. You're not gonna cause me any more problems, are you Drex?"

The kid shakes his head. "Boyd shouldn't have run off, especially as he was unarmed. He was usually one for obeying orders. If he'd done so, he'd be alive now."

If Drex is an imposter, I give him full marks for artistic impression. This change in character, if true, can only be a bonus. But I'm not about to take him off the suspect list. As for Boyd—what he did or didn't do, will now never be known. I'm just as much in the dark as I was before.

"I agree with Velez," Hewlis says, rubbing at his grizzled chin. "We need to be armed if we're gonna fight whatever is out there. None of us want to die like this. And my guess is that Boyd was targeted because he no longer had a gun."

"We have guns," I reply. "Don't make me use them prematurely."

"Quit the threats, okay?" Hewlis spits. "I'm getting sick of them."

"This is Vatic," says Xev before I can reply. "If anyone can sort out this can of fucking worms, he can. So, shut the fuck up and let him get on with it."

I'm impressed with Xev's confidence in me, despite what he told me about Esta.

"Okay," Velez says, "if that's the case… what do we do next? What's his big plan?"

"I say we off the chef and see if she is who she says she is," Xev says with a malicious grin. "Hell, for that matter, we could kill everyone."

Killing off the remaining suspects to see who reverts to who they really are is an attractive option, although it's one that isn't very practical. "Thanks for the idea, but no thanks. I need them alive to help me make sense of this mess and hopefully give me a way out of it. Klund," I bark. "You mentioned there was a general lab aboard ship."

The geek jumps before nodding. "Yeah. Why are you interested?"

I pull him aside, deciding to keep the hair I found a secret for now. "Think it could handle a few DNA tests?"

Understanding dawns across his face. He ponders for a moment before nodding enthusiastically. "I guess you want me to winkle out the imposter? Good move. We have an all-purpose geno-suite. And we would be safe in there. Safe against whatever killed Boyd."

"Where is it?"

"Six decks up."

Another journey up the staircase. I groan. I may die in less than an hour's time, but at least my cardio-vascular system will have had a good workout.

"Klund will lead us to his lab where we're going to hold up for a while," I announce.

"His lab?" Hewlis says. "What the hell for?"

"It's not a discussion," I remind him, holding up my gun. "Just a courtesy announcement."

spread

IT'S A long, slow climb up the staircase. A climb made longer by my mind that keeps returning to Xev's revelation. *To Esta.* Millions of my neurones and ganglia desperately trying to fire every which way they can, wanting to fill all my available thinking time. But now isn't the time to get overwhelmed. Instead, I try to focus on the investigation. In particular, a niggling feeling about Velez and Denny's plan that won't go away.

I'm an all or nothing guy and their scheme seems way too passive for my liking. Velez is strong-willed, passionate and fiery. There must be more to Pirella being aboard than just a shaming. My bet is Velez planned to kill Glaxtinian somehow. Shooting her in the gut with a buzz-gun would've achieved just that. But Velez didn't go to all that trouble recruiting an ambassador's daughter to not go through with her plan. And if she had shot Glaxtinian, why not say so? She'd already given herself a death sentence by admitting her role in smuggling Pirella aboard in a supposedly Neo-Dawn operation. Why not go the whole hog and admit she killed her, if that is what she did? The answer is a simple one—she wasn't responsible for the death of Boyd's mother.

Who the hell was?

Hewlis breathes heavily from the climb—even after a few flights, the man is red-faced and, I admit, I'm also winded. I give the order to rest and we all sit down on the twisting stairs. I go down to the below landing where Pirella stands with Rooba.

The Jen's large eyes widen in pleasure at my presence. I wave her away before she can say anything, leaving me on my own with Pirella. Above me, Xev sits behind Velez, chatting to Hewlis. Rooba joins Eric Klund, whose face reddens to match the colour of the Jen's skin. Drex squats against the wall, his unfocused eyes staring sullenly into the distance.

Pirella stands hunched over, her jumble of limbs weak and flaccid-looking, chin on chest, her face hidden by her long, curly hair.

We lean against the staircase rail.

"How are you holding up?" I ask, aware of Velez watching us from above.

Pirella says nothing.

I push back her hair to reveal a puffy, tear-ridden face. "I want you to tell me again about the plan you hatched with Denny and Velez."

"It's not how *she* told it," Pirella says, nodding towards Velez. "Denny loved me. Velez is lying. She has to be."

We both know she's fooling herself. The girl has been through a lot. Surviving a gassing that killed her lover and most of the crew only to find out she was being played. That is a lot to process. "Tell me more about Denny."

"I'd had other boyfriends. A lot of them. But he was different. More wise… *real,* you know what I mean? He understood me. Loved me."

"And it was his idea to get you aboard. To give your speech condemning the Company?"

She nods.

"Was it something you'd written yourself?"

"Denny did it for me. He was good with words."

"Tell me the last line of the speech."

"Why"

"Just do it. Like you are doing it for real."

"It was… *What I am doing will send a strong message to the Company. Neo-Dawn will do anything and everything it can to stop this evil regime.*"

Pirella's voice rings out clear and loud on the stairs and everyone turns their head to listen. Out of everybody, the girl's words have the most effect on Velez, whose eyes glitter and sparkle, her neck thrumming faster than I've seen it before. Her body is tense—like she is readying herself for escape, but there is nowhere for her to go on the stairwell, other than up. And she'd be easily caught by Xev and Hewlis.

"Denny said it was important that I gave the speech. Because of who I am," Pirella says.

I turn my attention back to the girl who is fingering the amber pendant hung around her neck. "Did Denny give you that?" I ask.

"Yes." She smiles at the memory.

Sudden movement out of the corner of my good

eye—Velez throwing herself to the floor, her hand darting into the pocket of her uniform—and a spike of alarm from *Ariadne's* mind.

I push Pirella as hard as I can over the staircase rail. Her face a mask of betrayal and confusion as she falls into the elevator shaft.

A bright silent flash and I'm buffeted by a terrific gust that lifts me up and throws me against the stairway wall, the steps crumpling underneath me. A crash and smash, and the elevator comes thundering past, falling towards the bottom of the ship in the artificial grav, trailing cables, whipping the guardrail which is splintered into deadly, flying shards.

I stumble to my feet. Xev and the others are strewn on what remains of the stairwell. My eyes penetrate the dust and murk to spot Velez trying to scramble away.

"Don't fucking move!" I shout, my voice muffled and faraway, like it belongs to someone else. "Or I'll blow your goddamn head off!"

aftermath

VELEZ STOPS dead in her tracks, her body sagging.

"Goddamn it!" The sound of my voice is distant under the whistling of my ears.

Velez and Denny had rigged Pirella with a spread-bomb. The pendant Denny gave to her. Not as destructive as a regular bomb but devastating in enclosed spaces. And small enough to smuggle aboard without tripping detectors. Whoever designed it was a goddamn genius. Shipboard security would've been aware of who Pirella was—an ambassador's daughter slumming it with a waiter may have raised an eyebrow or two—but she wouldn't have been regarded as a threat. Yet she brought aboard a bomb hung around her neck and Velez set the thing off...

Clever... but heartless and calculating.

Throwing Pirella over the railing was pure instinct. She was dead already. Dead as soon as she fell for that prick Denny. But I can't help feeling a stab of guilt. She's not the first innocent who has died to keep me alive. Not by a long shot. I have *Ariadne* to thank for the warning. I may be blinded by the ship's powerful empathy field, but *Ariadne* had felt Velez's intent. An intent the ship inadvertently passed onto me. One thing is for sure though, without her forewarning, I'd be dead.

"What the hell!" Xev groans, lurching back to his feet to balance on the edge of the smashed steps, becoming aware of nothing between him and the drop. "A goddamn fucking spread-bomb. Shit!" He stands back against the wall, covered in dust and debris, his eyes falling maliciously on Velez.

"Grab her!" I order.

Xev grasps Velez's arm, twisting her roughly around. The chef screams in pain, crumpling on what remains of the upper landing. Part of the destroyed guardrail pokes out of her left side like a broken steel dagger, blood staining her chef's whites red.

I make my way up the damaged stairwell that took the full force of the spread-bomb blast and drag a trembling Rooba to her feet. The Jen is covered in powder and bits of blasted stairway but appears uninjured. "You okay?"

Rooba says nothing, her doe-eyes wide and wired looking, staring past me at the destruction of the elevator shaft.

Hewlis is also uninjured as is Drex.

Klund stays on the floor, his eyes closed. "Eric," I say, kicking at him with my foot.

His eyes flick open, his expression one of horror. "What did you do?" he whispers.

"What he damn well had to," Xev answers for me.

"The girl... Pirella. You... *you pushed her over the rail!*" Drex says as if speaking from the confines of some terrible nightmare.

"It was straightforward self-preservation," Xev says in reply. "Vatic did what he had to do. Pirella was booby-trapped with a spread-bomb." He kicks at the chef. "And this bitch set it off."

"Velez?" Klund croaks, pushing himself up onto unsteady legs.

"Yeah," I answer, pointing towards the chef. "The pendant given to Pirella by Denny, her supposed boyfriend."

"That's just evil," Drex croaks, his eyes falling upon the chef. "Evil!"

"Let's get out of here, I say ignoring him.

We stumble into a corridor leading to one of the lower decks, Xev dragging a screaming, bleeding Velez like a carcass, and dumping her on the corridor floor.

A few moments later, my ears pop, although the whistling hasn't gone away. I remember the silver hairs I retrieved from Boyd's hand. I was holding them before the explosion. They're now gone. Lost somewhere in the stairwell. Damn!

I climb up to Velez. She lifts her head to stare at me with a dust-encrusted face, her expression showing pain at her injury—as well as fear and loathing.

"Is that what you were planning?" I ask her. "To blow Pirella and those VIPs in the Hospitality Suite to kingdom come?"

Velez's pulls herself up to sit against the corridor wall, her eyes momentarily closed in pain.

"Answer me!" I bark.

"You've seen that room," she croaks, more blood

leaking from her wound. "The plastiglass window. All that was needed was a small device." Velez coughs, a dry, hacking sound.

"That was a clever idea," Xev says jovially, as if getting almost blown up on a runaway spaceship was a fun day out for him. "For a terrorist that is. They're not the most imaginative folk. The best they can usually come up with is to point a buzz-gun and shoot. I'm actually fucking impressed."

The twitch in Velez's neck starts to thrum again, increasing in speed, her heart trying to fight the blood loss. "I told you, I'm not a terrorist," she gasps through the pain.

"Well, you sure act like one," Hewlis says, his voice a low, guttural growl.

I snort. "Velez and Denny planned it to make it look like a suicide attack. A speech against the Company followed by an explosion."

"That's some cold, cold shit," Xev says, shaking dust from his hair.

Velez's eyes dart down to her side and the blooming stain of blood now turning her whites almost fully crimson. "I think… I think I need help."

"With so much blood loss, she won't have long to live," Hewlis says.

"We can't let her die, just yet," I say. "Anyone here have medic training?"

Hewlis nods.

"Good. See what you can do to stop the bleeding."

While Hewlis checks over the wound, I turn my attention back to Velez. "How did you get the ship's schematics?" I ask her.

"I was contacted by the real Neo-Dawn," Velez croaks, wincing in pain from the engineer's touch. "They knew I had history with Glaxtinian. They told me about tonight's party and that she would be there. A red rag. They even supplied me with the spread bomb. A device small enough to put into the pendant Denny gave to Pirella."

"Did you meet this person from Neo-Dawn?"

The chef grimaces, her face becoming paler as the engineer's big hands press around her wound, blood leaking through his spatula-like fingers.

"Answer the damn question!"

"I didn't meet anyone," Velez finally replies, her once bright eyes dulling. "The instruction was to set the bomb off in the Hospitality Suite mid-party, with Glaxtinian and the other VIPs... I did everything I could to make that plan work. We were going to let Pirella act out our little fiction and then..." A small chuckle escapes her lips.

"Blow everyone up!" Drex blurts. "Including me and Boyd?"

"A neat plan," Velez continues, seemingly enjoying the kid's disdain. "Until everyone was gassed. We never got a chance to do what we came here for. And someone else killed that bitch Glaxtinian..."

I digest her words. Velez, Denny and Pirella were here to kill Glaxtinian under the guise of working for Neo-Dawn. Someone wanted them aboard *Ariadne* to do their dirty work for them. At least my hunch was right—Pirella giving a speech wasn't the full story. "Exploding that bomb in the elevator shaft was almost suicide."

"What other choice did she have?" Xev says.

"He's right," Velez spits, her breathing becoming laboured, the twitch in her neck now a frantic blur. "You're not going to get out of this mess, none of you are! And I was dead already, as soon as that brat ratted me out. I took my chance. If I survived, I was gonna head for the escape pods. Make or break."

Hewlis straightens and gets to his feet, wiping blood off his fingers with his oily rag and shaking his head.

"Velez is gonna fucking die on us?" Xev says disappointedly. "I was looking forward to offing the bitch."

"Fuck you!" Velez rasps. "You're all gonna be dead soon, dead and buried! All of—"

A shudder fills the chef's frame. Velez gives me a startled look, before her head slumps forward onto her chest and she lets out a final, rattling breath.

Hewlis checks her over. "Dead," he announces.

"And good riddance!" Drex says, going up to the chef and spitting on her.

"One thing is for sure, though," Xev says, disappointed, "Velez isn't a copy. Neither was Pirella."

Drex turns to stare at me. "I can't get over what you did to Pirella, I just can't."

"You think Pirella was innocent?" I reply. "Maybe she was. But I didn't kill her. That was Velez. All I did was save your goddamn hides."

"Yeah," Xev says. "Vatic is a goddamn hero." He shakes more dust out of his absurd hair, brushing at his velvet coat and ruffles. "That's two down and still no imposter. Which means it's either Drex, Klund,

Hewlis or Rooba."

"Or none of us," Rooba says, keeping her head turned away from my old boss.

Klund remains quiet, his expression distant, his mind elsewhere. I guess he's still trying to process what just happened. They all are.

"How the hell are we going to find out who it is?" Hewlis says, his eyes watery and red-lined. "You gonna kill everyone, like Xev suggested?"

"I have a plan," I reply.

"Of course you do," Xev says, the smile returning to his crooked lips, creasing over his over-whitened teeth—a nightmarish ghoul with perfect dentures.

I push past him and the still warm body of Velez. "C'mon, let's get out of here."

The corridor is full of dust from the explosion, grating at my throat. "Hewlis. You know this ship. With the stairs and elevator gone, how else can we get around?"

"Service tunnels, ladders and hatches," he replies, going to wipe the dust off his face with his now bloodied oily rag and changing his mind. "Why? You still want to go to Klund's lab? After what just happened?"

"Klund, come here!" I shout, ignoring him.

The geek looks up and rubs at his ears, coming back to himself. I wave him over with my gun and he complies, his dust-smeared face showing understanding, although I can see he's still in shock over Pirella's death and the explosion. He's a lab-type. The closest the guy gets to any action in the real world, is playing some dumb stream-game. Real life tends to hit people like him the hardest. I suppose for someone like Eric Klund, all this is a lot to take in.

"Show Hewlis where your lab is located."

After a quick chat with the geek, the engineer leads us away.

Rooba appears on my shoulder. She's still trembling.

"You okay?" I ask.

"What you did…" The Jen's voice falters.

"Hey, I did nothing other than to protect myself and everyone else. Are you telling me the Jen are not as ruthless as Velez and her supposed Neo-Dawn cell? That you've not killed a rival or a lover before?"

Rooba shakes her stylised head. "We are prepared to do anything and everything to get what we want when we get the chance. Everyone knows that about us. Consorting with the Jen comes with its own risks—*and rewards*. You did what you had to, I understand the reasons, but it doesn't mean I have to like them."

"I don't care what you think. I'll kill you just as easily if it comes to it. Just make sure you don't give me a reason."

Rooba stares at me for a few moments and smiles. "You're a good man, despite all your harsh words. I'm not an empath, but I can sense that in you."

"I'm about as far away from good as you can get."

The Jen draws breath to reply, but I raise a finger to my lips. "Don't try to play me, Rooba."

A few steps ahead, Hewlis stops in front of a service panel and pops it open.

"Everyone inside!" I order, waving my gun.

bloods

ANY WORRY that *Ariadne's* internal structure might be stuffed with more bio-matter or cooked flesh is quickly dispelled. The opening reveals nothing more than conventional electronics and mechanical components.

Hewlis squeezes his immense bulk inside and Xev follows—good. I need him at the front of the party. He knows his job. Judging by the amount of relish twisting his mangled face, I guess it's the first time in years my old boss has done anything important. And besides, he's not exactly the bastard I thought he was.

Drex, Klund and Rooba follow, with me bringing up the rear. I pull myself into the small tunnel, leaving the dust and debris-strewn corridor behind.

"Don't touch anything," Hewlis shouts from ahead. "The ship is in enough trouble without us messing with its systems."

I stumble forward, having to crouch in the cramped space. Rooba, with her impossibly long legs and cloven hooves, is forced to bend almost double. And suddenly, she is absurd, cartoonish. The Jen's allure comes from carefully contrived poses and stances to show off their attributes. Thrust into this service tunnel, she is nothing more than a series of long, red, awkward limbs.

After a few more minutes, we arrive at a ladder. Hewlis is already above us, climbing. I also start to ascend, although my legs are complaining. When I get off this ship and away from Stranng and the damn Company, I'm gonna get my body back to how it once was. I think about my plan to live as a farmer on the colony worlds—a dumb idea brain-squeezed into my head by Esta. As soon as I'm fit again, I will find her. A meeting that both excites and disturbs me.

We pass a range of hidden levels—service floors that exist between decks. Wires, hydraulics and various nodes and other tek that I've never seen before. I hear Xev say something above me, but he's muffled by the other bodies. When I climb higher, I understand what he was talking about. I've seen a lot of things in my time. Carnage, death, mutilation, and torture, but to see human flesh mangled into the infrastructure of *Ariadne* is truly disturbing. Nerves, muscle and other tissue is threaded throughout this layer, connecting directly to the ship's conventional systems. I reach out a finger and touch what appears to be a thick, stretched nerve.

I'm hit by sudden and sharp pain. But the pain is not mine. It belongs to the ship, to *Ariadne*.

Is she suffering? Has the damage inflicted by Klund on her environmental systems and the explosion in the elevator shaft injured her is some way? Can a ship like *Ariadne* even feel pain? Maybe I'm imagining it?

My fingers tingle and the nerve starts to twitch. It's alive, of course it is. This ship is made of bio-components. I've been aware of this since before I came aboard, but the reality?

A goddamn nightmare.

It's not an intellectual response, but something visceral. *Ariadne* is a perversion. I pull my hand away and wipe it against my skinsuit.

We emerge into a different ship section. Most of this deck is open. A vast lab with rooms and alcoves around the outside stretching as far as half the ship and surrounding a central pillar that houses the now destroyed elevator. At the far end of the deck are a series of desks, imposing lab equipment, and extensive and impressive-looking data stacks. The air in here is cool, no doubt kept at an artificially low temperature to the rest of the ship, accommodating the serious amount of computers and other equipment this deck is stuffed with. I also spot five dead bodies.

Hewlis whistles. "Wow! So, this is what the Company can do when it wants."

I'm similarly impressed and reminded of the Zeta-Karst Labs that I visited only a few days ago. A goddamn lifetime away. "You say there is no direct connection to *Ariadne's* mind?" I ask Klund. "I've never seen so many data-stacks aboard a ship."

The geek shrugs. "For diagnostics only," he replies. "The lab is temporary—and soon to be taken down. To be honest, we have done most of the work that was needed. All that biological matter we saw between decks is functioning as expected."

"Except that it's not is it? *Ariadne* is not functioning

as expected, is she?"

Klund shakes his head. "Yes and no," he says like a teacher patronising a slow child. "The ship's systems are just that. *Systems.* Some parts are mechanical or bio-mechanical, while others are entirely biological. But all are controlled and monitored by *Ariadne.*"

Back on home ground, Klund is more confident and assured. His voice loses some of its whiny quality—in its place? Something akin to pride.

"*Ariadne* is a prototype brain," he continues, "implanted inside this space vehicle very much in the same way we might get inside an exo like a cargo loader. Of course, *Ariadne* has a more direct connection—via the ship's infrastructure and neural pathways—but the principal is just the same."

"What do you know about exoskeletons?" I ask the geek, reminded of the ventilation shaft where the body-blank was hidden and the ripped remains of Boyd. An exo could've been used for both.

"I can't operate one, if that's what you're asking," Klund replies. "But you get my point about *Ariadne*?"

"Okay," I reply irritably. "We already know you worked on the ship's bio-mechanical systems. Do you have any way of contacting *Ariadne*? Her mind?"

Klund shakes his elongated head. "We teks never had direct contact with the ship's consciousness. As far as I can tell, Chandrasekhar was the only one communicating with her. The professor wanted her to learn. Wanted her to watch and understand human behaviour. If anyone has a chance of communicating with the ship, that someone is you."

"Me?" I reply aware of everyone staring.

"*Ariadne* is an augmented mind," the geek continues. "Genetically tweaked and containing the empathy gene. She is a Skilled, like yourself. Can you sense her? Can you feel *Ariadne*?"

I nod, wondering why Klund is bringing this up again.

"You can feel the goddamn ship?" Xev blurts. "What the hell is *Ariadne* saying to you?"

"Nothing," I reply. "All I can sense is her madness. An empathic wail. And too loud to make any sense of."

Klund laughs, a thin, weird sound.

"What's so fucking funny?" Xev says, walking up to the geek, putting his face in front of his.

"It is something Chandrasekhar wrote," Klund replies without missing a beat.

"And what the hell was that?" Xev asks.

"That what he was creating here was far superior to the Skilled. An evolutionary step upwards. His words, not mine."

"I don't care what the professor wrote," I reply. "We have more pressing concerns. Where are the gene sequencers?"

"This way," Klund says with a shrug, and walks towards the end of the lab.

"Sequencers?" Hewlis repeats. "Huh?"

"I think that's obvious," Xev says. "Vatic is gonna test us. Our DNA. He's going to root out the bad guy here and now. And about time. I'm getting pissed off with not knowing who it is."

"You and me both," Hewlis replies.

Their eyes turn towards Drex and Rooba.

"It ain't me," Drex says.

The Jen shrugs and says nothing.

Klund leads everyone to a data-bank near the back of the expansive laboratory where sits some quite impressive machinery, complete with dials, buttons and flashing lights. I wouldn't know a gene-sequencer if it bit me. The geek makes himself busy, while the others look on.

I nod to Xev. "You know what to do."

My old boss goes up to Rooba and roughly pulls out a few of her red hairs. If it hurts, the pain doesn't register on her doe face. He does the same to Drex and Hewlis before approaching Klund—who pulls out one of his own short blonde hairs from his almost shaven scalp with a pair of tweezers.

"You might as well test me, while you're at it," I say. "And don't forget Xev. Better to be safe than sorry."

"Agreed," Xev says, "but this ain't my real hair," he adds with a flash of his mangled smile. He snatches at an eyebrow and pulls away a couple of follicles and passes them to Klund. "They needed a fucking trim."

The geek makes a show of placing the hairs into six separate containers, marking them *Vatic, Xev, Hewlis, Drex, Klund* and *Rooba*. He shows them to me to make sure he hasn't done anything underhand. I'm no scientist, but everything looks as it should be and Hewlis nods. The geek slots the containers into one of the machines, pressing a couple of buttons.

"How long?" I ask him.

"Minutes," he replies, crossing his arms.

I turn to everyone else. "Anyone want to own up now?"

Silence.

"Keep an eye on them, Xev," I say. "Call me over when the results come through."

"On it," Xev replies with relish, levelling his gun at the others.

I bring up my wafer and start checking the bodies I spotted earlier. All dead from gassing. Nothing to see here, other than these guys were at the top of their game—juniors, but with some quite impressive credentials. My mind goes back to Velez. Her death irritates me. Sure, she deserved to die from detonating a bomb meant to kill Pirella, me and the others, but with her gone, I can't interrogate her.

And I really needed to know... *who contacted her and why?*

Could it have been a play from Glaxtinian? If anyone knew about Velez's antagonism, it was her. To become an Arbiter in the Company hierarchy meant she must've had a ruthless streak. And a pretty strong one at that. Did she arrange to get Velez aboard by masquerading as Neo-Dawn? A terrorist cell being found aboard the *Ariadne* would certainly have undermined Professor Chandrasekhar and his project. Glaxtinian could've exposed Velez, enhancing her reputation and making the transition of power over this project a smoother one. Or she could've been trying to get Chandrasekhar out of the picture altogether. Blowing him out of the ship with the other grandees would've certainly achieved that. But Chandrasekhar was an asset—like it or not, he came up with this ship and the cereb, *Ariadne.*

If true, that's quite some play from Glaxtinian.

And a real possibility.

But of course, Velez could've been contacted by the real Neo-Dawn. Taking out a roomful of Company VIPs would certainly be a major success for them. But something Xev said resonated with me. *Terrorists are not particularly imaginative.* The plan sounds too complicated for them. Which leads me to believe someone else is involved. And whoever created that tiny spread-bomb was a genius.

My thoughts turn towards the ship-wide gassing...

Could *Ariadne* have been responsible for killing the crew? She sure seems insane enough for such an action. The little I have felt from her seems to back this up. If so, what caused her insanity? A failure in the experiment, perhaps? Or was it simply an over-reaction to the onboard murder or the threat of Velez and her associates? Did *Ariadne* sense the attack and, in trying to nullify it, take out the entire crew?

At this point, anything is possible. I check the time on my wafer.

23:32

Twenty-eight minutes to go. Or thereabouts. The imprecise nature of this mission only adds to my sense of unease. I like to be in control of things, of people... of the goddamn job.

At least I can now find out if the imposter is one of the survivors. And if not? How the hell am I going to stop this ship?

There is one possibility. A possibility with as little chance of success as Velez's spread-bomb. I've kept it as the last and final option… Someone must get outside the ship and blow the Snag Array.

Suicidal.

That would bring the ship out of hyperspace, sure, but at what cost? We'd return to normal space with a bang. *Ariadne* wouldn't survive. Not in one piece that is. She'd break up like any other ship.

When I'm done checking the bodies, I walk back to the others who are anxiously awaiting the DNA results. "How are we doing?" I ask Klund.

"Nearly there… a few more seconds," he replies, looking up from his data-centre.

"What kinda shit are we trying to find?" Xev asks, pointing the gun at what I'm guessing is the genome sequencer.

"The imposter will give a dual report," the geek replies. "Two types of DNA. Although it will also pick up any unusual nanite or cellular activity."

A beep from Klund's data-centre and lines of information appear on its screen. He steps back to let me look.

Sample name: 'Vatic'.
Genome: Empath.
DNA augmentation: Skilled

"No surprises there," Xev blurts. "Except that it doesn't mention what a bastard you are."

Sample name: 'Xev'.
Genome: Human male.
DNA augmentation: None.

Evidence of thirteen Juvo treatments.
Evidence of extensive DNA damage and cellular decay.

"That's as close as a clean bill of health as I'll ever get," Xev says with a chuckle.

Sample name: 'Eric Klund'
Genome: Human male.
DNA augmentation: None.
History of brain augmentation and illegal intelligence boosters.

Xev claps Klund on the shoulder. "Haha. I knew you brain-boxes were just as bent as the rest of us. Intelligence boosters? You fraud!"

Xev then turns to Hewlis, Drex and Rooba. "Starting to sweat?"

Sample name 'Drex'.
Genome: Human male.
DNA augmentation: None.

"I'm a good guy," Drex says with a relieved sigh.

"You doubted yourself?" I ask.

"A little bit," he replies, smiling.

I raise my gun at Rooba and Hewlis who swap glances with one another. "Just you two left. If you're gonna reveal yourself, now would be the time." They remain silent.

Sample name 'Hewlis Gray'.
Genome: Human male.

DNA augmentation: None.
History of bone and circulatory system augmentation.

"Get down on your knees!" I shout at Rooba.

"No way!" she says. "It's not me! This is a goddamn set up!"

Drex jumps forward, his fists raised. "If you had anything to do with Boyd's death, I'll kill you myself."

Sample name 'Rooba Jen'.
Genome: Multiple detected.
DNA augmentation: Extensive.
Evidence of DNA suppression.
Evidence of extensive cellular and nanite activity.

I push Rooba down onto her knees. The Jen doesn't resist. "Get something to bind her hands," I say to Klund.

For a moment all he does is stare.

"Don't make me tell you again."

The geek fumbles around in a drawer and produces a roll of tape. He gives it to Xev, who wraps it tightly around the Jen's thin, red wrists.

Rooba says nothing, acting passively while the engineer binds her.

"What's the plan?" Xev asks me, a nasty glint in his eye. "Interrogate this fucker until she fesses up?"

"I say we off her now!" Drex blurts. "They revert when they're dead, yes? Let's see who she really is!"

"No more murder," I bark, angrily.

"Why the hell not!" Drex shouts.

"Because she might know what has gone down

on this damn death ship, that's why," I reply. "I'm gonna find out what she knows, before anyone does anything."

Drex lurches at Rooba. I knock him to the floor with a rough elbow to his guts. As he draws breath to complain, a deep rumble comes from somewhere below, shaking the ship, the sound becoming louder.

"Shit!" Xev blurts as the elevator doors are blown inward, filling the deck with fire and smoke.

scream

THE FORCE of the blast throws us all to the deck, alarms blaring accompanied by red flashing lights. The ship is vibrating—the deck, the bulkheads and everything inside. My assessment? *This ain't good.*

"What in space was that?" Drex blurts, pulling himself off the floor, rubbing his gut where I elbowed him.

I turn to Hewlis. "What the kid said. And don't you dare shrug."

The engineer pulls out his wafer, taps it and reveals red flashing schematics and readouts. "Shit! The spread-bomb caused a rupture in one of the main ship coolant systems. The explosion blew out the lower hydroponics deck. It's totally gone. Blasted into space. Which means…"

"Let me see that!" Klund says, snatching the wafer off the engineer, his thin fingers quickly navigating through screen after screen. Relief crosses the geek's face. "The Snag Array appears to be unaffected. Hydroponics is gone and the deck above it has depressurised. Vacuum has entered the elevator shaft and stairwell. The rest of the ship seems undamaged, although there is sure to be a knock-on effect to other systems."

"Automatic hatches and panels have shut, so we're safe from depressurisation," Hewlis says, grabbing his wafer back from Klund's weak fingers.

"With Hydroponics destroyed, how long will the air last?" I ask.

"Longer than it will take for *Ariadne* to reach enemy space," Hewlis replies. "Although I think we should all suit up when we get the chance. Just in case."

"We have to somehow get this ship out of hyperspace and quick," I say. "Hewlis, you're supposed to be an engineer. With no direct access to the bridge or any control systems, is there any other way of disabling the Snag Array, without blowing the thing up? Because that's seriously looking like our only goddamn option."

The engineer's eyes widen, as if what I've said has sparked an idea. He rubs a hand over his grizzled chin. "Maybe we can blow the Array, or at least part of it," he says, his eyes darting at his wafer, his sausage-like fingers tapping quickly at the screen.

"But that's suicide!" Klund says.

"You're not listening," Hewlis replies, a look of hope on his face. "Vatic said 'disable'." He holds up his wafer to show us a series of flashing schematics. Technical stuff that makes no sense to me.

"What the hell is that?" says Xev. "Explain."

"It's an automated emergency damage report," Hewlis replies. "I don't normally work on hyperspace systems, but in ship-wide emergencies like this one, protocols are enacted to share damage information. All Company ships systems are triple protected from attack. In particular, engine and hyperspace systems. The ability to jump away from trouble in an emergency is paramount to a ship's survival. Like the bridge, the systems are protected by some serious bulkheads, however, hyperspace arrays are vulnerable. They have to sit outside the ship. But not on the *Ariadne*. She can retract her array. Protecting it from attack. My guess is that is how she jumps in and out of hyperspace. If we can somehow get her legs to retract into the fuselage then—"

"Then we can maybe stop the goddamn ship before we reach the border... before Strang blows her up."

Hewlis smiles. "Because of all the secrecy aboard *Ariadne*, I had no idea about how the array was deployed until I read this damage report just now. It sure is sweet."

Xev rubs at his head. "You're saying that fucking explosion may have just saved our goddamn lives?"

Hewlis nods. "We blow the mechanism that keeps the legs extended and they should retract automatically, collapsing the hyperspace field. Dropping us back into normal space rather than throwing us out of it—which would be disastrous."

"You told us earlier that you only work on the convention sub-light engines," Klund says. "How can you know this will work?"

"And you're just the geek who makes sure the ship's bio-mechanical connections are in the green," Hewlis snaps at him. "Do you have a better way out of this mess?"

Klund is agitated, annoyed. His long, thin head shaking in frustration—I guess he's a fan of convention, of rules and regulations, of doing things the accepted way. Thinking outside the box is difficult for him. "How do you plan to do it?"

"It won't be easy," says Hewlis, "and I'm not one-hundred percent sure it will work. Someone goes outside the ship, plants an explosive and gets the hell out of there."

Xev taps Hewlis on the shoulder. "It sounds to me like you're that someone."

"'Fraid not," Hewlis replies stabbing a thick finger at his wafer. "Whoever does this will have to be slim enough to squeeze through these leg stanchions. There's no way I can do it. It will have to be one of you."

"I'll do it," says Drex.

"You sure?" Hewlis replies. "Once the legs are retracted, it'll be a rough ride back into normal space. You'll need to anchor yourself to the ship."

"Hell, I'm dead already if we don't do this. We all are. And if I pull it off, it'll look great on my record, so why not?"

"Rather you than me, kid," Xev says. "But good on you."

"Before we do anything, we need to find out who this imposter is," Klund says. "Isn't that why we are here in my lab? To find out what they know? Maybe Rooba has a way of stopping the ship?"

"I don't know anything," Rooba says quietly. "I've been set up." She darts accusing eyes at Klund. "I'm not the imposter. You've all been played."

"You all saw me do the tests," Klund says, raising his hands. "There is no way I could have manipulated the results. You have been caught fair and square young lady."

"It seems to me like we have a choice," Hewlis says. "Interrogate this bitch in the hope she will give us a way out of this mess, that she can somehow command the ship to leave hyperspace, or we take more direct action."

"Go with the engineer's plan," Rooba says. "I know nothing about the goddamn hyperdrive! I'm a consort. You've all been duped. Blowing the array is a better proposal than wasting your valuable time talking to me."

Drex roughly kicks Rooba, making her grunt in pain. "I say we off her now. Blast her six tits all over the deck."

All eyes turn to me.

"Time is running out," I quickly say. "Our best option is action. We go with Hewlis' plan."

"Then we might as well kill it now!" Drex says.

"Do it!" Rooba replies. "At least you'll know I'm innocent."

"No!" I reply. "No one else is gonna die. Not on my watch. Not unless I deem it's necessary."

Drex is not pleased, but he ain't the one in charge.

"Where do we need to go?" I ask Hewlis. "Cos we need to go now."

The engineer taps at his schematic. "Not far. Two decks below. Follow me."

Hewlis steps towards the open panel and stops

in his tracks. From the depths of the ship, comes an inhuman wail, a soulless, terrifying sound, full of ominous tones and primeval threat.

"What the hell is that?" Hewlis says.

"I don't know," Xev replies. "But it sure sounds pissed off."

I make eye contact with my old boss. "You think that sound came from the thing that tore Boyd apart?"

Xev chuckles darkly. "If we weren't in enough trouble as it is, something is in the walls and it ain't happy." He grabs Rooba and roughly pulls her to her feet. "You're with me, honey," he says, dragging her towards the open panel. "If there's something down there, maybe they'll go for you first."

I glimpse Rooba's face, the snouted mouth is closed, the eyes unreadable. My estimation is that she's shut down. Switched off. "Keep a close eye on her," I say to Xev. "We have no idea what we're dealing with. She's dangerous. She may even be in cahoots with that thing down there."

"I know," Xev replies. "That's why I've got this antique fucking buzz-gun stuck in her back. She won't be able to do much anything with a hole blown in her spine." He jabs the gun at Rooba. "Are you listening, sister?"

Rooba doesn't react.

Xev looks inside the door panel. "Nothing," he says, pushing Rooba before him.

Hewlis turns his big mop head toward me and Xev, his wet eyes staring intently from the brown skin of his weary face. "And make sure to have your guns ready, should they be needed. I don't want to end up like Boyd."

"None of us do," Drex says.

airlock

WE EMERGE into the freezing darkness of two decks below, lit only by the engineer's wafer, which reveals a cramped corridor, walls the same brass metal as the bridge area, but featureless. The cold leeches into me. I pull back the blood from my extremities, but it doesn't stop the chill.

"These are the bulkheads that protect the hyperspace array," Hewlis says, staring at his wafer, his voice a low rumble. "Impenetrable. But, our plan ain't to try and break in."

"We didn't search down here," Drex says. "I didn't even know it was an actual deck."

"It isn't," says Hewlis. "This is the cavity that houses the array when it's retracted."

Drex looks startled. "You mean that if the array is closed, we'll be crushed?"

"That ain't gonna happen," Hewlis replies, "… yet."

Xev makes a guttural snort. "You sure know how to pep-talk," he says. "Maybe you can tell us your thoughts on that thing we heard screaming down here. You think it's coming to get us?"

"Shut up, all of you," I say. "Let's get a move on before we all freeze to goddamn death."

We walk forward in the dark—crazy shadows flicking on walls, floor and ceiling. Xev's words and the memory of that dreadful scream have me worried. Something is down here with us. But what? I become convinced I can hear the pad of heavy feet somewhere behind.

I hang back, buzz-gun in hand, the circle of light leaving me as the others keep moving. Without the light, the cold feels suddenly magnified. I concentrate on my ears. On nothing else. A trick I learned a long time ago. Moving my head from side to side. But with the ship vibration and various other mechanical noises coming from behind the bulkheads, I'm hard-pushed to hear anything.

"Vatic! Where the hell are you?"

The voice belongs to Xev.

"Here," I shout, jogging back to the others.

"What the fuck were you doing?" he says.

"Let's get on," I reply.

We arrive at an air-lock area. Hewlis punches a switch and the chamber is flooded with light. An ante-room large enough to house a series of tools, skinsuits and helmets and the six remaining survivors that now occupy it. The door is made of the same thick, brass-like metal as the bulkheads.

Xev thrusts Rooba onto the floor, keeping the gun pointed at her. Playing the 'guard' with aplomb.

"What do I have to do?" Drex asks, his voice nothing more than a squeak. The kid is afraid, but

I give him his dues. What he's about to do is damn brave.

"You need to crawl down the outer hull," Hewlis replies, rooting through tool bins and hatches. "The array field fluctuates, but never touches the ship. To stay safe, you'll need to keep yourself away from it, otherwise…"

"Yeah," Xev says smirking "You don't want to lose your head like Boyd."

Drex flashes Xev an angry look.

"Hey," Xev replies. "I'm just trying to get you to focus on the job."

"What you're looking for," Hewlis continues, ignoring the exchange, his eyebrows furrowing over his wafer, "is the control node where the central leg emerges from the fuselage."

"That sounds straightforward," Drex replies.

"It is, kid. You can't miss it." The engineer straightens, his hands grasping a welding torch and a canister of hull sealant. "It's the next bit that's tricky." He hands the torch to Drex who takes it off him, a determined expression on his face. "What do I need this for?"

"You will have to squeeze through the leg-stanchion to get to the node. Once there, attach yourself securely and burn a hole inside. You'll see a whole heap of wires. Just keep burning through them. When you've made a hole as big as your head, fill it with the hull sealant. Once deployed, it will begin to quickly expand—dangerous stuff in an enclosed environment. Which is your cue to try and get back inside the ship. The node should be ripped apart, forcing the legs to retract."

"Are you sure it will work?" says Klund, looking a deathly shade of blue in the cold.

The engineer's breath freezes upon the air. "Nothing is sure, but it's the only plan we've got."

"Yeah," Xev says. "Shut the fuck up and let the kid get on with it."

"I find the node," Drex repeats, focusing in on his task. "Burn a hole in it. Fill it with sealant… And head back to the airlock, right? And if I can't make it in time, to tether myself to the fuselage."

"Yeah. That's the plan," the burly engineer replies. "Talk to me over the two-way, relay to me what you see. But what we're attempting is straightforward, just unpredictable and a tad dangerous."

"Right," says Drex, who looks even smaller as he quickly undresses down to his boxers, his short, stocky limbs covered in goose bumps. He pulls on a skinsuit, tweaking its environment controls before grabbing at a helmet and entering the airlock. "Wish me luck."

Hewlis pushes the door shut and recycles the air. The outer-lock opens and we're bathed in the flashing lights of hyperspace.

"*It sure is pretty,*" Drex says over the com.

"Focus on the job. You see the central leg?" Hewlis says.

"*Yeah,*" Drex answers.

"Good. Make sure you stay away from the hyperspace field, or you'll be ripped apart."

"*I don't need telling that.*"

"Be careful and you'll be home dry."

"*I see the legs. I'll have to clamber over the hull to get to the node."*

"You're doing good kid."

"Shit!"

"What is it?" Hewlis asks, his large brown eyes staring at us.

"Some kind of gas emission, it nearly blew me into space."

"What do you mean?"

"Something vented from the ship."

"That can't be right," Hewlis says, bringing up his schematic. "There's a series of small ports and ducts all over the fuselage. There's no reason why any of them should be expelling gas."

"Could it be Velez's goddamn explosion?" Xev asks.

"No. The hull systems are isolated. I haven't a clue what that was. Drex… you okay?"

"Yeah, yeah. Took me by surprise."

"Just watch your step."

"I'm fine, I'm nearly there. Just a few more—aaargh! Fuck!"

"Drex what is it."

"Something hit me. Debris."

"Drex, anchor yourself to the ship now!"

"Where the hell would debris come from?" I ask.

"It's *Ariadne*," Klund says. "I knew it! She does not want us to succeed."

"What the hell do you mean by that?"

"I told you… she has gone insane."

"I'm gonna anchor myself… I can't take the chance that—"

"Drex?" Hewlis shouts down the com.

Static.

"Drex! Come in."

"I'm loose. I'm gonna hit the hyperspace field. I'm gonna—"

"Drex!" Hewlis repeats. "Drex!"

No reply other than the repeated crackle of the com.

Xev hunches his shoulders and shrugs. "Drex is dust," he says. "Goddamn it!"

I turn to Hewlis, who's face is a pallid blank. "What the hell did he do wrong?"

"Nothing," the engineer replies, his eyes on the outer-lock door.

"It was *Ariadne*," Klund rasps. "She did it."

"But how?" Xev asks.

Hewlis pulls one enormous hand through his curly grey hair and grimaces. "Like I said, I'm just a regular engineer. I don't know how *Ariadne's* systems interact with the ship."

"She could do it any number of ways," Klund says. "Vent a port, super-warm or super-cool the outer hull to interfere with a skinsuit, blow an inspection hatch."

"Then why didn't you warn Drex before?" Xev asks in exasperation. "We just sent that kid to his death."

Klund shrugs. "I did not realise how much the ship wanted to kill us."

"Well guess what," I say. "Seeing as you know all about it, you're up next. Get suited."

Klund is motionless.

"You deaf?" I reply. "Maybe *Ariadne* won't want to kill you as much."

"But I'm not trained in evac," he bleats. "And besides, this is a stupid plan."

I turn to Hewlis. "Basic Training is still Basic Training, isn't it?"

The engineer nods. "Company policy. Has been since the war."

"So, you're all trained-up, Klund. What are you waiting for?"

The geek says nothing.

"Speak!" I shout at him.

A deafening scream from the corridor outside the airlock and a massive, muscled silver-haired, blood-splattered creature careens into the room, crashing into me.

giri

THE CREATURE knocks me to the floor—the wind blasted from my lungs—and a rough, powerful hand wrenches the buzz-gun from my belt.

The thing shrieks loudly, and I see the monster for what it is. *A humanzee.* Half-man, half-chimp. The *old-faced boy* Pirella was so insistent she'd seen. The monster that ripped Boyd apart and that had been following us ever since Klund joined our little band.

Xev raises his gun, but is too slow, the creature knocks it from his hand. It clatters along the floor towards Klund.

The geek scrabbles at the gun with long fingers, scooping it up.

"Shoot!" Xev shouts, but the geek does nothing. "Klund! What the hell are you waiting for? Blow it away!"

A sly smile appears on Klund's lips. "Stand down, Giri," he says to the humanzee, his voice full of sudden authority. "And give me that bastard's gun."

The creature called Giri comes back to itself, the anger and threat leaving its face, unable to resist the words of who I now know is its master. It turns on enormous, flattened, naked feet and hands my gun to Klund.

"Thanks," the geek says, with a pleased grin, stuffing the weapon into his belt and raising the other against me, its decorated exterior flashing in the harsh light of the airlock chamber. "Get up, Vatic and meet Giri. My faithful companion for many years." He turns to the humanzee and smiles. "You did well, my friend."

Giri sidles up to Klund and takes position at his side. It wears a one-piece bloodied smock that fits tightly over its stocky, overtly-muscled frame. I remember Boyd's ripped limbs and shudder. This creature must have the same strength as a chimpanzee—but he's twice the size.

"I could've saved myself a lot of trouble if I'd instructed Giri to kill you," Klund says to me. "But I told him to keep the Skilled alive. That was my first mistake."

I stand up and glare at the geek. "So, what's your next move… *Professor Chandrasekhar?*"

"What?" says Hewlis.

"Oh well done, Professor!" Xev says, clapping his hands, keeping one eye on the humanzee. "I knew you were a smart cookie. But this is off the chart."

Professor Chandrasekhar, aka Eric Klund, smiles. "This was my show from the start," he begins, a practiced sneer crossing his youthful, elongated face. "My ship. My project. All mine. And the Company wanted to take it away from me, didn't they? To give it to my supposed successor, *Mandibald Glaxtinian*. They should've realised who they were dealing with. I knew Glaxtinian was up to something when I found out her son, Murton Boyd, was aboard gathering intel to try and bring me down. *Me!* You think I haven't survived similar coups?"

He produces a small punch-syringe and jabs it into his neck. Almost instantly, the geek's facial muscles begin to twitch, accompanied by a growing darkness to his skin.

"I'm one-hundred and sixty-two years old," Klund continues. "How do you think I got to this great age whilst keeping my vaulted position in the Company? By sitting back? By letting the ambitious walk all over me? By letting them steal my work?" His face puckers into an old man's scowl. "No. I've survived many Company coups in my time and this one is no different. Sure, it's messier than I would've liked, but the Company will get the message that I'm not so easily replaced. Nor underestimated."

"So, what exactly went down here?" I ask. "About Glaxtinian, Neo-Dawn and this goddamn gassed ship?"

Klund takes a step back and smiles. "My plan was simple if not audacious. I organised the party under the guise of presenting *Ariadne* to the Company, knowing that Glaxtinian was going to use this event as an opportunity to take control. But the jumped-up arbiter underestimated me, as many have done before... all to their disadvantage. Yes, it was I who contacted Velez and gave her the idea and the means to blow Glaxtinian and all those other self-important grandees into space. The ship's strategist, a career-minded girl who had gotten too big for her boots and who was beginning to undermine my authority, was to take the blame—after myself and *Ariadne* saved the day by killing Velez and her associates of course. Increasing my personal stock with the Company whilst getting back full control of my project."

His face droops while he is speaking, deep lines revealed in his cheeks and forehead, the colour in his eyes draining away, like blue water swirling down a plughole.

"My plan was to wait until the supposed Neo-Dawn attack, resulting in the death of Glaxtinian and the other VIPs," Klund continues. "And then to *neutralise* Velez and her associates. Neat, clean and easy."

"But why poison the rest of the ship, why gas everybody?" Hewlis asks, unable to take his eyes off Giri.

"Because the professor messed up," I say. "It was you, Chandrasekhar, who shot Mandibald Glaxtinian, wasn't it?"

Klund becomes more stooped, his shoulders shrinking, his clothes baggy, revealing a smaller, but well-defined physique. His skin has reverted to a liver-spotted brown, the short blond hair of his scalp reabsorbed to leave a naked, shiny pate. The man is compact, and despite his great age, he seems to be in good shape. Intense, with no little power. Eric Klund is now gone I realise, fully replaced by Professor Chandrasekhar.

"Mandibald Glaxtinian was a player," he says. "She not only wanted to take over my project but to undermine me... to rub her victory in my face. We were on the way to the party—before which, I would be *unavoidably called away*—and she came out with it. Told me there and then to make the most of the event, because as far as she was concerned, *it was over for me*. Until I produced my trusty buzz-gun."

Chandrasekhar waves the decorated gun at me, a glint sparking in his now brown, hateful eyes.

"Glaxtinian made a few bleats," Chandrasekhar continues, a smile flicking across his almost lipless mouth. "You know the kind of thing—the noises made by those egos that can't believe someone is actually going to shoot them hard in the gut in front of everybody. To be honest, that's what pushed me to do it. You should've seen the look on her surprised face as I disintegrated her stomach. I went back to my cabin and enacted my back-up plan. I sent an encoded, pre-programmed message to rival space, instructed *Ariadne* to cut all coms, lock the bridge and to jump into hyperspace."

"But heading towards rival space is a suicidal move," Xev says. "You'll never make it."

The professor lets out a small laugh. "Don't be a fool. I will order *Ariadne* to drop out of hyperspace before we reach the border, where…" he pauses, as if to give his next words more import, "we will be met by enemy battleships to escort me the rest of the way to their territory and to destroy any Company ships that might try to stop me!"

Xev laughs dryly. "So, this ship isn't out of control after all. It's all part of your fucking escape plan."

"And everyone else was expendable!" Hewlis spits. "You're quite the asshole."

Professor Chandrasekhar shrugs. "The enemy company wants me, my ship and my research. After I shot Glaxtinian, I decided on taking up their generous offer. Only my work matters to me, nothing else. As for prisoners? That would be too messy. I ordered *Ariadne* to gas the ship. At least the crew died quickly and easily."

"But not everyone died, did they?" I say.

"That was *Ariadne's* doing," the professor sneers. "She wasn't happy with the crew being killed. *Her friends* is what she called them. *Her family. Ariadne's* systems pervade this ship… or they did. She rebelled, locking me in Hydroponics and venting the air. But Giri and I don't die that easily. I was able to override most of her systems, to keep control of the ship, although I later found out she'd cauterised half of her living circuits to stop me gassing anyone else."

"The burnt flesh of the air-con," Hewlis says.

I feel an uncommon rage, but this is not my emotion. It's *Ariadne*—a spike in her general sense of mania. I now realise why she is so distraught. Not only was she forced to gas the crew, she'd cauterised her own living flesh. No wonder she went insane. The anger might come from the Cereb, but I feel it like my own.

"*Ariadne* is powerful, but she is still just a child," Chandrasekhar continues, proudly. "Still learning her place in the world. I made sure to have full control over her mind, no matter how much she tried to resist. I built her so that she would be obedient."

"Locking you in hydroponics and burning her own systems doesn't sound like obedience," I say.

"Seems like she was trying to prevent you killing more people."

"It doesn't matter what she thinks," the professor says, glancing at the humanzee. "And besides, no one knew my little friend was aboard. Giri has been with me all his life. But while we were trying to escape… *you arrived, Vatic*. I must admit, I didn't expect the Company to react so quickly. And sending in a *Skilled* was unexpected. But I'm nothing if I can't improvise. I patched myself into the ship's coms and cameras and watched you come aboard. Watched when *Ariadne* let you out of the goddamn airlock before frying the cam-feed and blinding me. I made her pay for that. Put her in excruciating pain."

"I never guessed *Ariadne* was helping me. All this time, I assumed she was the enemy."

"While *Ariadne* is under my control, she still is your enemy, fool! Although she's been railing against me ever since the crew died. But *Ariadne* is not expendable. I was too soft with her. I gave her too much emotion. It made her unstable. Her replacement will have more backbone. I'll make sure of that from the start."

"I don't get it," says Rooba, squatting on the airlock floor. "If you're in control of this goddamn ship, why the disguise? Why pretend to be one of the survivors?"

"Vatic getting aboard *Ariadne*, irked me. A goddamn Skilled! What if *Ariadne* was somehow able to communicate with him about Chandrasekhar, about me? What if Vatic found out I was still alive and was responsible for what happened on this ship? I wanted to discover what he knew and how much of a threat he represented. I couldn't possibly confront him as the professor, so I took on the ID of one of my juniors who I knew very well. *Eric Klund.* He survived due to the air filtration system in his cabin and came to find me. A mistake. I took his identity to get close to Vatic, to blow off one of his legs and incapacitate him. The enemy would be very pleased to get their hands on a Company empath, especially after what Vatic did in the war. An extra bonus. But he took my prized gun before I had a chance to use it and I was forced to join your pathetic little band."

"And you ordered that vile creature of yours to murder Boyd!" Hewlis says, speaking up.

The professor gives a shrug. "My instructions were for Giri to keep only Vatic alive. The rest of the survivors were fair game... if he should come across any of them unarmed. Giri is a faithful servant but has little in the way of imagination."

"Masquerading as Klund was a neat disguise," Xev says. "You fooled us all. Even Vatic. Although that isn't a first."

I ignore the dig from my old boss. "You must've been desperate to use such a dangerous transformation?"

Chandrasekhar shakes his head. "I invented the procedure for the war. My genius. Since then, I have substantially enhanced the technique. My disguise took a lot of energy—and I will pay for that later. But it's always worth a little suffering to come out on top, don't you think? And things worked themselves out in my favour as I knew they would. *They always do.* Although I was unprepared for Velez's attack. I was lucky to survive. But luck is one of my greatest allies.

It was also luck you came aboard, Vatic. Even if you have been somewhat of a pain. The enemy will be impressed that I've brought a Skilled along with my ship. Two prizes for the price of one." He flicks the gun in my direction. "Give me your wafer."

I unzip my skinsuit and hand it to him. Chandrasekhar grabs it with a hand of thin, translucent skin covered in liver spots.

I guess he's had most of his organs regenerated or substituted. There's no doubt he's had some work done to keep him alive this long, but I can see no evidence of cosmetic procedures. No, this man wears his age like a badge of honour. I've seen the infirmity of geriatrics at first hand. The smell of it. The closeness to death that shines out from behind cloudy eyes, but not so with Chandrasekhar. He is full of life. Despite his looks, his brown eyes sparkle.

He stares at the readout for a second, before addressing us again. "I have eighteen minutes before we reach enemy space, before your friend, Stranng, will open fire," he says, dropping the wafer onto the floor and crushing it underfoot. "But I will bring the ship out of hyperspace before then. I have a rendezvous to get to, remember?"

"*You?* You will bring the ship out of hyperspace?" Hewlis says.

Chandrasekhar gives him an angry look. "I control the hyperdrive, remember? Via a direct connection to *Ariadne*. We arrive shortly. Imagine the shock on your Strategist's face when he comes up against a phalanx of enemy warships."

"And what about us, about me?" Rooba says.

"You think it was hard for me to fix that little test back in the lab, implicating you? Child's play. But let me answer your question. You're not going to make it. None of you are."

"You're gonna kill us in cold blood like you did Mandibald Glaxtinian?" Rooba says with incredulity. The Jen are an arrogant breed. I guess this isn't a possibility she'd ever considered.

Chandrasekhar nods, taking a deep breath. "I'm afraid everyone is going to have to die, apart from Vatic and myself."

"Everyone?" I say, flicking my eyes at the blood-covered humanzee. "What about your pet?"

"I'm afraid he's not coming with me. Giri has been a faithful servant but his usefulness is now at an end. He's getting old and, besides, the enemy company have promised me the ways and means to create superior pets. And out in the open, not secretly behind closed doors like I have to do with the Company. As such... he will regrettably have to be sacrificed." Chandrasekhar stands back and waves the gun at Giri. "Join the others!"

Giri remains motionless, its primitive mind slowly working out the intention of its master. The humanzee's face goes from confusion, to horror, to rage.

"Get back, Giri," Chandrasekhar says calmly, but the creature ignores him.

I can't empathically read the humanzee, yet I can easily see the turmoil creasing its tortured face. The creature makes a series of low hooting noises, its head shaking from side to side, its massive hands bunching into twin, agitated fists.

"You've served me well, Giri, but everything has to come to an end," the professor says with a hint of sadness.

Giri opens its powerful maw, revealing terrifying fanged teeth, and growls with primordial threat.

"Don't come any closer!" Chandrasekhar warns, taking a few steps backwards and pointing his buzz-gun at the creature's head.

The humanzee follows him, thumping its chest.

"Giri! I'm warning you!"

The creature lurches forward.

Chandrasekhar pulls the trigger, but there is no resounding crack and bang of a buzz-gun. The professor pulls the trigger a second and a third time. He fumbles with the other gun stuck in his belt, pulling it out just as Giri shrieks and leaps onto him, plunging his teeth into the professor's neck, fangs cutting easily and deeply into the ancient, sallow flesh. With a wrench of his head, Giri rips out Chandrasekhar's throat.

The professor grabs at his neck, blood pumping from ripped arteries, an incredulous look on his face, before falling dead onto the airlock floor.

Giri turns back to us, its chest and body stained with thick, fresh blood, its fists curling again in anger. Hooting and wailing. I also feel a jolt from *Ariadne*. I push her back from my mind.

"Don't do it, Giri," I say, forcing command into my tone. "You're like me. A product of the same genetic interference that birthed my breed. Hell, it's possible that the same DNA running through the human part of you is the same as mine!"

The humanzee pauses for a second, as it considers my words, and I glimpse the human within the animal.

"You are as much a victim of the professor as *Ariadne,* as are all of us," I say, raising my voice. "Stand down!"

Giri shakes its head, grunting and hooting, and beating at its chest again.

From out the corner of my eye I see a darting movement. Rooba throws herself against the creature's legs, barrelling into them.

The humanzee is sturdy enough to keep its feet. Feet that stamp down on the Jen, who dodges impossibly quickly.

I use this opportunity to roll to the floor towards the rack of supply bins, and grab at the first thing that comes to hand. A can of hull sealant.

Hewlis raises his right hand, his fingers tapping nervously together, his face covered in sweat. Standing his ground in front of this monster.

I have to act now, before it's too late…

Giri kicks Rooba aside, slamming the Jen into the airlock wall with enough force to render her unconscious. The creature screams, raising itself onto large, flattened feet, beating its chest and throwing back its head, screeching and howling like some weird primeval demon. I jump to my feet and, in the same movement, throw myself at the creature, wrapping one arm around its mammoth head, and stabbing the can of hull sealant into its wide maw.

Giri instinctively bites down. The can explodes, filling the creature's mouth with a thick, grey foam that quickly expands, pouring out of its mouth and nostrils. It gurgles and rasps in pain before its head finally bursts open with a crack and the spray of blood and brains. The humanzee falls dead to the airlock floor, twitching and shaking.

implant

"HOW IS Rooba?" I say to a shocked Hewlis and Xev. The Jen lies on the floor, groaning.

"I'm okay," she croaks, coming around. "Just a little stunned." She sits up and baulks at the dead bodies of Chandrasekhar and his unfortunate humanzee, Giri.

"Why didn't Chandrasekhar's gun work?" Hewlis asks, unable to keep his eyes off Giri's sealant and blood-covered corpse.

"You think I'd be dumb enough to give a charged weapon to Xev? I'm a Skilled, remember, I ain't stupid."

"And neither am I," Xev replies. "I knew my gun didn't have a charge."

"But why?" Rooba asks.

"He wanted to flush out the bad guy," Xev answers.

"That's right," I say. "Look at Xev. He's old, past it and half-drunk. I figured if someone wanted a gun bad enough, they might try and take it off him."

Xev pulls a pained expression. "Thanks. But it's what I also figured. Even if the gun was loaded, I didn't stand a chance against that Giri creature. Shit!

He came out of nowhere!"

"Yeah, I didn't know what was following us until it was too goddamn late. The thing went straight for my gun. It may not have been intelligent, but it worked out who was the biggest threat."

A white-faced Hewlis crouches over the body of the professor and peers closely into the gaping wound in his ripped throat. "I'm no medic," he says, "but there's something in here that looks like a bio-implant powered by his nervous system." He pokes at the mangled flesh with a large stubby finger. "I think it's a communication device, but unlike anything I've seen before."

"It must be how the professor was controlling *Ariadne*," I say, making the obvious connection. "By direct thought command."

"That's a sick idea," Hewlis says, his voice shaking. "*Ariadne* is a human mind. No one should be allowed to control someone else like that."

"She's a prototype Cereb," I reply. "*Ariadne's* mind was unstable. And we know that Chandrasekhar was a controller."

"My guess is that he made her too human," Hewlis says. "That's why she fought back against him. Rebelled after he killed the crew by frying her own systems and releasing you from the airlock, and by trying to lock the professor in hydroponics."

"To be forced to kill her friends... that would send anyone insane," Rooba says, pushing herself onto long slender legs to stand towering above me, blood matting the fur on her brow in a darker shade of crimson.

"Yeah," Xev spits, releasing the Jen from her bonds. "Chandrasekhar held all the cards. He must've commanded *Ariadne* to try and kill Drex to prevent the ship exiting hyperspace too early. Drex was going to his death and he let it happen."

Hewlis wipes his bloody finger on his overalls. "And with the professor dead, there's no way for him to order *Ariadne* to drop out of hyperspace. Which means…"

"Which means someone else has to go out the airlock to disable the Snag Drive array," I say, finishing his sentence. "I'll do the job myself. With time running out, I have to do it now."

Hewlis nods, his mop of grey curls sticking to the sweat of his face. "Do you think the professor's orders still stand? Do you think *Ariadne* will also try and kill you?"

"There's one way to find out."

The burly engineer takes a deep breath. "You know what you've got to do?"

I nod. "Find the node, burn a hole in it. Fill it with sealant… and retire to a safe distance. And I'm done, right?"

Hewlis nods in return.

I grab a helmet and enter the airlock. Rooba comes up to me, her big eyes full of pride. "Good luck," she says.

"I'm Vatic, luck doesn't come into it," I reply, pushing her away. "And stop trying to play me, it won't work."

"I mean it," she replies. "I want to live. You're my only chance."

I grab another can of sealant and a burn-torch and strap them to my belt. The airlock closes behind me. A hiss of air, the tightening of my skin-suit, and the outer door slides open.

snagged

I'M HIT by the dazzling spectacle of hyperspace. Blobs of light streak past me, some the size of specks of dust, others as big as the stars themselves, each trailing light as twisting, iridescent gossamer tails. There's no substance to these apparitions, or that's what the scientists say. No reason for this lightshow that they can base in physics. Maybe they're the universe's thoughts, sparking and flashing as the great entity ponders? There have been many explanations for what I'm seeing first-hand. But they have never concerned me. I'm practical, I live in the moment. It's a pretty distraction and that is all. Thousands of years of study has not revealed what the universe is or why we are here.

And I don't care.

My only concern now is to collapse the hyperspace array without *Ariadne* getting in the way. And if she couldn't stop herself killing Drex, she could still kill me.

A sudden spike of warning from *Ariadne,* and a port below vents a gas of some kind. It freezes instantly into a jet of frozen particles. An attempt to sandblast my skinsuit and knock me into space. I have just enough time to twist myself out of the way.

Ariadne is trying to help me, I realise. Something she couldn't do for Drex, which means I have an advantage…

The glowing legs of the Snag Array stretch over a hundred feet away from the bulbous fuselage. Their tips disappearing in and out of existence as they ride the hyperspace wake. Eerily silent. Beautiful—if I cared about such things. I concentrate on the now. *Ariadne* will have more surprises for me along the way if I attempt to crawl along the outer hull. There is only one thing for it—to ride the *Wake*.

The Snag Array pushes *Ariadne* forwards, like the prow of an ancient water ship, creating a sizable wake around herself. If I were to jump away from the ship, the wake would pick me up and fling me out behind her, my body ripped apart by the same eddies and currents I successfully navigated to get aboard.

I will need some way to stop myself from being 'washed away'. Drex had the same idea. He tried to latch himself onto the fuselage using the umbilicals. Self-deploying tethers found outside the airlock and at regular points along the ship's skin. But something went wrong. Did *Ariadne* deliberately untether him, so that he fell into the wake? It seems a likely possibility.

I will need another way to anchor myself. But how? The only option is to roll the dice and hope I can grab a hold onto one of the leg stanchions as I fly past them. At this point, I can't see any other option.

Damn!

Another warning from *Ariadne*. A section of the outer fuselage—an inspection hatch the size of a sewer grate—is blasted outwards. It gets caught by the wake and flies straight at me. I flatten myself on the hull and it misses by inches. I want to thank *Ariadne*, but her mind is still too powerful, too disjointed and confused. Psychologically damaged beyond repair.

I shake my head, pushing *Ariadne* away. Whatever I have to do, I have to do it now. I'm about to take my chances and jump untethered into the wake when I notice pipes and wires spilling from the recently blasted, open hatch in *Ariadne's* fuselage. I crawl quickly over to it, ripping the tubes and wiring free and tying them to my wrists and ankles, spreading out from me like roots in a zero-grav hydroponics bay. Giving me a way of latching on to the Snag Array.

Another section of the fuselage is blown, and again *Ariadne* warns me. I let the debris fly past and launch myself behind it, trailing wires, tubes and flexi-pipes like the tentacles of some strange space creature. I'm floating roughly ten feet above the ship, but the wake is pushing me higher. I can't afford to get too far away, otherwise I'll sail straight past the array and into the hyperspace field—like what happened to poor Drex. I do the only thing I can do. An emergency procedure. I command the suit's nanofibres to vent a small amount of air, before quickly closing again, a burst of gas pushing me downwards. The legs of the vast Snag Array fly towards me at speed and, with a gasp of terror, I realise I'm still too high. I vent more air, but it's hopeless.

I'm going to sail right past the array and into the

hyperspace wake!

A trailing wire on my ankle snags on one of the upturned stanchions and I'm suddenly floundering, twisting and turning—like a fish on the end of a line. I quickly grab a hold of the wire and reel myself in, inches away from the Hyperspace field that would rip me into so many disparate atoms.

I goddamn made it!

I take a few moments to curb the frantic beating of my heart and orientate myself, spotting the control node on the central leg. I use the burn torch to cut myself free of the entangled wires and pull myself through a series of tight connecting struts until I'm hovering over the small boxlike structure. I use the burn torch a second time to create a small opening, and thrust the can of sealant deeply inside, programming it to deploy in thirty seconds.

I pull myself back along the central leg towards the ship. If I'm successful, and the legs retract, *Ariadne* will smoothly enter normal space. And I need to be as close to the ship as possible.

Twenty seconds. Ten. Five. Four, three, two, one…

The node explodes silently behind me, and I feel a stab of emotion akin to sorrow from *Ariadne*. She was aiding me, and yet I sense she didn't want to be stopped.

Did she want to die?

I have little time to ponder. The legs begin to retract, folding in on themselves. I'm hit from behind by a collapsing strut, it knocks me forwards, slamming me into the fuselage. I scrabble to find a handhold, but it's too late. The hyperspace field collapses and

I'm spun backwards, forwards and inside out before smashing face-first into a wall of blackness.

empaths

"WELCOME BACK, buddy!"

I open my eyes.

Strategist Stranng is standing above me, his eyes glinting. "Seems like you only went and goddamn did it."

I'm lying on a bunk in the ship's tiny, but functional medibay, Shereena looking down at me with concern, her face full of apology. She wants to speak but can't seem to find the words. She betrayed me and is full of guilt and sorrow. It radiates from her in massive waves until I realise those emotions are not coming from Shereena, but from *Ariadne*.

"How is he?" Stranng says.

Shereena tilts her head to one side. "Beat up, bruised, and still emaciated. But he's okay."

"What happened?" I croak at Stranng.

The Strategist ignores me.

"Speak to me! That's a goddamn order!"

"Talking of orders," he says, rather too pleased with himself. "I've recently been informed that your rank as a member of the Secondary Executive has been unfortunately rescinded by the Company. Seems like they wanted me back in charge, and I'm not about to argue with them. Which means you don't tell me what to do ever again, you get me?"

I take in the information with an annoyed nod of my head. "How did I get here? The last thing I remember is disabling the Snag Array."

"You sure saved the day," Stranng replies. "I was itching to blow you outta hyperspace, you sure cut it close. But you did it. Demoted or not, that's quite an achievement."

"But how?"

"We picked you up floating alongside the *Ariadne*," Stranng replies.

"What in space were you doing outside the ship when you re-entered normal space?" Shereena asks me. "We thought you hadn't made it. That was very lucky."

"Luck had nothing to do with it," I snap back at her. "What about the others?"

"The survivors are being ferried back as we speak," Stranng barks. "Three people out of a contingent of forty-three ain't a good percentage. The *Ariadne* was in total shutdown when the rescue crew boarded her. All systems dead. I've been ordered to leave her out there until a specialist team turns up. Which suits me down to the ground."

"Her systems are dead?" I feel for *Ariadne* again. She's still there, although I sense something else. A desperate desire for freedom. For escape. And something else. Something dark and threatening.

"Dead as space," Stranng answers. "What the hell

happened over there?”

“I’ll put it all in my report,” I reply. “Not that the Company will give a damn. But we have more important concerns. You need to take me to the bridge, now!”

“Didn’t you hear me? You’re not my superior any more. You don’t tell me what to do. Quite the damn opposite! Hell, I might even decide to throw you out of the airlock again, just for old times’ sake.”

“Listen, Stranng, there are enemy battleships out there waiting for *Ariadne* to turn up. They were to rendezvous with Professor Chandrasekhar. He was behind what happened aboard and was planning to defect.”

“Enemy battleships? Shit!”

“Yeah. And *Ariadne* is not as dead as you think. I can still sense her mind. She could pose a danger to this ship.”

“What?”

“She’s an empath like me. You need me Stranng. Now are you gonna take me to the bridge or what?”

Stranng stares at me with his piggy eyes and makes the intelligent decision. “Okay. Come with me.”

I slide off the bunk, pausing only to swap a few quiet words with Shereena.

“You two can make up later,” Stranng barks at me.

The command crew jumps to attention as we enter the bridge. The sense of loyalty to their commander is cloying, as is their intense dislike. I wish I could block their feelings, but I need my empathic abilities to listen to *Ariadne*.

I glance up at the bridge-wide screen that stretches from floor to ceiling, like one enormous window, and see her hanging in space. Without her hyperspace array deployed, *Ariadne* is nothing more than an elegantly shaped blob. At this distance, she is no longer the invasive force in my mind she once was. I feel a sense of guilt from her—betrayal, self-loathing and pain. And behind those emotions? A dangerous and unpredictable sense of desolation.

"You say that bioship isn't as dead as we think?" Stranng says, looking at me. "Tactical, get our weapons online and ready. I don't want to be—"

"Multiple incoming void-points opening, sir," the woman on the navcom replies.

Stranng juts his fat head towards the screen as five ships appear.

"Warship class, sir," the woman continues, a wobble in her voice. "Enemy designation."

"Shit! Seems like you were right," Stranng says to me with a grim smile. "Patch me in to them."

The woman operating the navcom nods. Stranng draws breath to speak, no doubt to warn the enemy ships that they are in Company territory. His words are cut off by a series of bridge alarms.

"The lead ship is powering weapons, sir," says a white-faced tactical officer. "She's putting herself between us and the *Ariadne*."

"Get us out of here, Stranng!" I say. "We're done for."

"I can't," he replies. "I have direct orders to protect the *Ariadne* until support ships arrive.

"There's no way to do that now!"

"My orders are to—"

"Fuck your orders! We're out classed and out-matched. The Company ain't worth dying for!"

Strnng shakes his head. "Enemy ship," he begins in his familiar belligerent tone. "You are in Company space. Stand down and leave our territory immediately."

More alarms.

"We're being targeted, sir," says the tactical officer, his voice trembling. "Multiple locks."

"Evasive manoeuvres, now!" Strnng orders as the ship's engines thunder into life. "Fire everything we've got."

The bridge is rocked by the thrum and thud of our ship's mag-rail cannons and lasers. The dampening field kicks in a few seconds later to protect the crew from the sudden increase in grav as the ship lurches.

I keep my eye on the screen that now shows a tactical display. The lead battleship still has a target lock. We'll be blown into dust in moments.

A stab of anger mixed with intense hatred.

It's coming from *Ariadne* and so strong that I'm forced to close my mind to it again.

"The *Ariadne* has come back online, sir," the girl on the navcom says. "All her systems are powering up."

The lead enemy battleship blooms into a hole of white light. Behind it is *Ariadne*, her mag-rails already slamming into the second ship that also explodes into a blinding star. The three other ships converge on the *Ariadne*, concentrating their fire upon her. Three against one is odds no ship can win against, and yet

Ariadne survives, flitting this way and that. A third ship is destroyed and then a fourth. The fifth ship's Snag Array begins to glow, trying to escape, but it doesn't have the time and disintegrates in a hail of laser and mag-rail fire.

"Who the hell is flying that ship?" Stranng spits, sweat dripping from his face.

"No one," I reply. "It's a bioship, remember? The Cereb, *Ariadne,* is back in full control."

"Shit! Thank space the enemy didn't get their hands on her," Stranng says in relief. A relief that also washes over the bridge crew. "That ship is a goddamn marvel!"

I can't help but agree with Stranng. If the professor needed a demonstration of his work, of what a Cereb was able to achieve against regular battle computers, this was it. The man was a genius, if not insane. Except that all is not well with his creation. The anger coming from *Ariadne* abruptly changes back to one of unremitting desolation. An emotion now stronger than all others put together. It floods through me like hard radiation, crashing into my molecules and smashing them apart.

And this time, I let *Ariadne* flow through me. I could never have done this while I was aboard her. I was too close to the bright beacon of her Skilled mind. I'm suddenly overcome with the same desolation that inhabits her. She is full of grief. Grief at what she was forced to do, killing the crew she had grown to love. Forced into that murder by her father who she had grown to despise. And another emotion. *Kindredness.*

She recognises me for what I am.

Not the same but similar. This is why she stopped Stranng's ship from being destroyed.

I am her brother…

"What the hell is wrong with you?" Stranng barks.

I come back to myself, aware of tears streaming down my face. Not my tears, but *Ariadne's*, and in that moment, I know what she is about to do.

"*Ariadne* is powering her weapons again, sir," the tactical officer says.

"Stand down, *Ariadne!*" Stranng orders, fear stretching at the edges of his voice. "Can she hear me, can that damn ship hear me?"

"She won't harm us," I say. "I can guarantee you that!"

"We haven't got a chance anyway," Stranng says. "Fire everything we've got!"

Don't do it, Ariadne!

The words scream out of my mind directly towards the Cereb.

I'm an empath, which allows me to feel what others are feeling, to understand them at an intimate level. But to never talk to them, or another Skilled, mind to mind. And yet *Ariadne* somehow hears my words and replies to them.

I must! Ariadne broadcasts into my thoughts.

The voice leaves me as suddenly as it arrived. *Ariadne* does not want to harm me or this ship, she simply wants to die. And already it is too late.

I open my eyes to see *Ariadne* on the screen, multiple points along her rounded hull explode under the fire from our ship's mag-rails and lasers. They combine to create more explosions until her engine core is exposed and she is blown into a bright shining star of dust and debris.

bio

"VATIC!"

I open my eye to see Hewlis standing over me. I sit up and find myself back in the medic bay. Rooba lies on the bed next to me, a medical pad attached atop her peculiarly-shaped head. I automatically search for *Ariadne*. But she's gone. My mind probing the hole she has left in my consciousness like a tongue searching for a missing tooth.

"What am I doing here?" I croak, rubbing at my head.

"A couple of medics dumped you on a bunk a few minutes ago," Hewlis says, sitting down on a chair. "You were out like a light."

"Where's Shereena?"

"Shereena?" Rooba says. "The Triple Bar Patron?"

I nod. "You noticed that too, huh?"

"The first thing I always notice is rank. Don't forget, I'm a Jen." Rooba's long-lashed eyes flick to the thick, heavy door. "A Patron acting as a ship's medic? She must've pissed off someone high up in the Company."

"Where is she?" I repeat.

"She left with Xev to go see Stranng. He managed to convince the MPs to get a message to him. I think he wanted to explain how he personally caught a Neo-Dawn terrorist."

"And you didn't go with them? It's unlike the Jen to miss an opportunity for advancement."

"The medic wouldn't let me. Something about the concussion I received when that Giri creature tried to bash my head in. And besides, it was you who got us out of that mess, not him."

"I hope Shereena has been looking after you both properly?"

"She sure has," Rooba replies. "Gave us all a proper physical and a whole series of shots."

I wince at the memory of my harsh extraction from hypersleep and the many injections I was subjected to. "She is a medic at the top of her game. And very thorough."

"And... *very sexy*," Rooba replies.

I also remember Shereena's betrayal. Drugging me to allow Stranng to send me over to the *Ariadne*. "You should pursue her. She's just your type. You'd get along like a house on fire."

"What was all the commotion?" Hewlis asks. "I'm guessing with all that mag-rail and laser fire, there was some kind of ship-to-ship altercation?" He looks worn out.

"Those enemy ships of Chandrasekhar's turned up," I reply.

"They did?" The engineer says, his eyes widening.

"*Ariadne* attacked them, destroying them all."

He whistles.

"And then she attacked this ship," I continue.

Hewlis furrows his bushy eyebrows. "Then why aren't *we* destroyed?"

I shake my head. "You heard the professor. *Ariadne* wasn't the ship we thought she was. He was controlling her, making her do things she didn't want to do. *Trapped.* In the end, she took back control and took her own life. Call it *assisted suicide.*"

And good riddance!" Hewlis replies. "Some things shouldn't be allowed to live."

"You never were a fan of *Ariadne,* were you?"

"Like I said, there was a bad feeling aboard her. And after what went down over there, I wasn't proved wrong."

"Is it true you've been demoted?" Rooba asks me.

"Yeah."

A wave of disappointment emanates from the Jen. I guess she was lining up her ambitions on the back of a member of the Secondary Executive named Vatic.

She gives me an annoyed look. "And that doesn't bother you?"

There's no way she can fathom how I feel about the Company, or about my role in the war. No one can. No one except the Skilled. "I want nothing to do with the Company ever again," I say. "Hell, I've been trying to escape them for years."

"You have?" says Hewlis with genuine surprise. "But you were one of the grandees. A goddamn member of the Second Executive."

"An honorary title that's been thankfully taken away."

"So, what are you now?" Rooba asks. "Your rank, I mean?"

I shrug. "I am what I always was and what I've always been... a *Skilled*. That's all the rank I'll ever need." I push myself to my feet and realise I'm a little shaky. I go over to Hewlis and look him in the eyes. "What do you really think about the Skilled?" I ask sharply.

"Something up?" he says. "You seem a little... off."

"Just answer the question."

"You're like *Ariadne*," he replies, and I sense he's controlling himself. "Another Company human experiment."

"That's true," I reply. "And who or what are you?"

Rooba's confusion enters my mind. She's perplexed by the way I'm talking to the engineer. But I'm only just starting.

Hewlis draws breath to reply.

"And don't lie," I say. "I know you're not who you pretend to be..."

Rooba places a delicate, long-fingered hand upon her snouted chin. "What?"

Hewlis says nothing for a few moments, his face a perfect mask of confusion. "Did you also get bashed on the head?" he says, a jovial slant to his tone. "You sure look serious."

I set my jaw, pushing my teeth together, my words a growl from the back of my throat. "I'm always serious, or didn't you get that about me?"

"Vatic, I have no idea what you're—"

"Do me the courtesy of telling me the goddamn truth!"

Hewlis becomes suddenly very still.

I sense the engineer's mind becoming ordered, relaxed. No longer working on the pretence of his identity. His shoulders go to shrug, but he stops himself. "How did you guess?" he finally says. "I've been in the presence of other Skilled before with no problems."

"What is this?" Rooba says.

"Your disguise is a good one," I continue, ignoring the Jen. "Very good. Most of what I sense from you, *is you*... Whoever you really are. When lying, it's always best to fly as close to the truth as you can manage. And you might've gotten away with it. But what let you down wasn't your ability to hide from me in plain sight—instead, it was something far more basic. All those ships you've been on. All those years of supposed experience. And yet you lacked the equivalent engineering knowledge. That's what alerted me to you. A real engineer wouldn't have wasted his time trying to break into *Ariadne's* bridge with Boyd and Drex. A real engineer would've told them straight-off that it was impossible. You may know a few rudimentaries to perform routine ship maintenance and you've an engineer's background from somewhere, just enough for you to keep your cover without raising suspicion, but I sensed there was something wrong with you from the start."

"If you thought that, why did you trust me. Why didn't you out me earlier?"

"I wasn't sure who you were or what your agenda was. Not everyone hiding in plain sight is a villain. Some are just hiding from Company punishment, some escaping an older, less successful life. As a Skilled, you get to notice these people from time to time. I ignore them. Leave them be. *Mostly.* It was difficult for me to use my empathic skills aboard the *Ariadne,* but the Skilled are more than that single trick. Sure, we rely on being able to sense someone's intentions directly, but when that skill is unavailable, the subconscious takes over. Creating that question mark I mentioned before. I was looking for an imposter, and I thought it was you for a long time. But there was a positive vibe from you, Hewlis. All the way through this. You've been on my side. You've been wanting to help me. But it was nothing more than pure survival. You knew I was the only one who could get you out of the mess aboard *Ariadne.* And you did everything to help me— because you wanted to help yourself, because, like me, you're also a survivor."

Hewlis says nothing, his expression far too calm for my liking.

"Velez, Pirella and Denny, might've been pretending to be Neo-Dawn," I say, "but it's you, isn't it? You had been on the *Ariadne* for weeks. Ever since you heard of the VIP party. Preparing your own terrorist plan. Even my Company wafer had your details. That's impressive cover. I guess you came aboard the *Ariadne* with the intention of sabotage, or even murder."

The pseudo-engineer's face becomes more confident and, if there's one thing I find dangerous about cornering a suspect, its sensing they feel they have the upper hand. And there's another emotion inside of him. *Desolation.* The same feeling I recently experienced from *Ariadne,* now repeated within the pseudo-engineer.

"What if I did?" he says. "Did you like what Chandrasekhar was doing? Did you like what he did to *Ariadne?* To that poor humanzee, Giri? I suspect you didn't. I also suspect that you're not really happy with what the Company did to you. To the Skilled. They manufactured you just like *Ariadne.*"

Rooba makes an audible gasp at my side. Again, I ignore her.

I notice Hewlis's hand, the fingers barely tapping together, like I observed back in the airlock when Chandrasekhar's humanzee was about to kill everyone.

"The genome is sacred, Vatic," he says, almost with triumph. "And you, like all the Company's genetic creations are an atrocity that must be destroyed!"

The flesh of his right arm twists and unfurls, the bones snapping and readjusting, rearranging themselves into what looks like a sizeable lump of conjoined flesh.

Hewlis grunts in pain, although his eyes remain fixed upon me. "You think that only those disgusting Jen know about body augmentation? Well think again! Sometimes you have to use the weapons of evil to fight evil!" He glares at me, his face full of manic fervour.

"What is that?" I say calmly.

He raises his arm. "This is a powerful explosive. Enough to take out this entire fucking ship."

Rooba shouts in panic, clambering off the bed and running towards the locked door, beating against it, screaming and shouting to be let out.

"A suicide attack doesn't seem like your style," I say unfazed.

"Chandrasekhar had a back-up plan," Hewlis continues. "A way to escape. Well, he's not alone. I also have a back-up. A way to get myself out of any mess I may find myself in… *permanently*. But yes, I always preferred survival, whenever possible. To strike at the Company as many times as I could until I was caught. I came aboard the *Ariadne* with the intention to act. I had planned a ship-wide failure that would've tragically resulted in the destruction of *Ariadne* and everyone aboard during that VIP party, including that bastard Chandrasekhar, my main target. Until I got aboard that is and realised the ship was way out of my understanding. My plan then was to lie low and get off *Ariadne* as soon as the opportunity arose. But now… you've cornered me. I have no choice but to do what I'm going to do!"

Hatred, sacrifice and the desire to kill rises inside Hewlis like lava in an exploding volcano.

"Death to the Company!" he shouts as Rooba squeals.

His arm jerks, but nothing happens. It jerks a second and a third time.

The hatred in the man disappears with the sudden realisation that he's been played. That he's been caught.

"How dumb do you take me for?" I ask.

The door bursts open and in walks Xev and Shereena with two MPs and a very pleased-looking Strategist Stranng.

"The medic!" Hewlis croaks. "Those… *those goddam shots!*"

"Yes," Shereena says. "Vatic warned me about you. Told me that you were very likely hiding a bio-weapon somewhere inside your body. Those shots contained powerful neutralising agents."

"But how did you know about it?" Hewlis says to me. "How did you find that out?"

"For a start, you were far too quick to spot the bio-augmentation of Professor Chandrasekhar after Giri ripped his throat out. That was quite some catch for a lowly engineer who supposedly didn't have any idea about bio-systems. And of course, there was your DNA test result generously offered to me by Eric Klund. What did it say? *History of bone and circulatory system augmentation.* It wasn't difficult to put two and two together. I guessed that if you were indeed Neo-Dawn, you'd have a similar bio-weapon, activated by the tapping of your fingers, as I observed you attempting before I killed Giri. How better to end your life in a destructive explosion using the 'foul weaponry' of your enemy? A bio-bomb is a specialist and expensive augmentation. Where the hell did you get it?"

"It makes no difference!" Stranng barks. "I've cornered and caught a Neo-Dawn terrorist."

"With the direct help of Xev Tranth, of course," Xev says, a smile plastered over the thick skin of his juvo-mangled face.

"And aided by the ship's medic," Shereena adds forcefully.

"It will take considerable spin to explain why the Strategist was forced to destroy the *Ariadne*," Xev continues. "But spin is my business."

Stranng nods. "And how I single-handedly destroyed those enemy battleships. I was up to my ears in this ass-mess, but hey, sometimes there's light even at the end of the most shit-filled tunnel."

Hewlis says nothing, I sense him shutting down. He's been caught. And depending on how long the Company wants to drag it out, Hewlis will be doing the naked dance outside an airlock near here sometime soon.

"Take him away!" Stranng orders as two MPs roughly grab Hewlis. "And you, Vatic, you're dismissed. Go to your cabin and get out of my goddamn sight!"

I give Hewlis one final look, and nod at Xev, who's face displays some of its old power. This was the lucky break he was hoping for. And I don't begrudge him that. Not one little bit. Even if I do hate the nasty, sneaky bastard.

"I said get out!" Stranng barks again.

shereena

SOMETIME LATER, Shereena, the ship's over-qualified medic, enters my room on the obvious pretence of getting me to report back to the medic bay for a series of tests and more shots to help my continued recovery from overlong hypersleep—which she informs me was the reason I probably passed out on the bridge, although her expression tells me she thinks there's more to it than that and, of course, she's right. Death to an empath is a disturbing thing, although I'm now cold to it, but *Ariadne* dying had been an experience I never want to repeat again.

"You gonna say nothing about what you did to me?" I ask her. "Crawling into my bed with the intention of knocking me out? That was a low move."

She reddens. "I didn't have a choice. You know Stranng. The man's a brute. He's gonna do well out of this," she says with even more guilt. "And so will I. I've been stuck on this ship in the back end of nowhere for too long. Catching that terrorist shithead is going to get me out of here and back where I belong."

"You're a survivor. So is Stranng and Xev, my

old boss. Survival is all that matters in this damn existence."

Shereena sighs and I sense she wants more from me than this conversation.

"About last night. Before your adventure aboard the *Ariadne*. I didn't need any orders from Stranng to come and visit you, okay? I… would've turned up anyway."

"You are saying what I think you're saying?"

She pulls herself up to her full height. "I like you, Vatic, and I'm not ashamed to admit it."

"Hasn't Rooba Jen made her move on you yet"

Shereena reddens again. "She has, yes. But I was thinking. Maybe when we get back to Earth, we can—"

"Thank you for the offer, but no thanks."

The impact of my words hits Shereena with a visible jot. I don't need no empathy to see I've stung her.

"But I had no choice! You know that!"

The image of Esta flicks into my mind. And I'm filled again with the desire to go and find and confront her. "I have other things to do."

"But afterwards…?"

I put my face close to hers, glaring at her. "Don't you understand who and what I am? I'm Vatic, and no one ever crosses me twice."

Reviews

If you enjoyed reading *Shattered Web,* can I ask you to please leave a review. This is not just for me and other readers, but for a whole host of other boring marketing reasons that I won't go into right now.

Suffice it to say, if you leave me a review on any of the e-book stores, or Goodreads or anywhere else, I'll be *well-chuffed,* and it will certainly increase the likelihood of further novels in this and other series.

Thanks in advance!

For information on further releases, please join my newsletter *http://mostlywriting.com/join*

Or you can pop over to my Mostly Readers Facebook Group (*https://www.facebook.com/groups/ mostlyreaders*). It's a friendly fun place to hang out.

Please read on for full details.

About *Shattered Web*

Writing *Shattered Web* has been a real effort of will. What do they say about that difficult second album? It's all true! I wanted to give up on quite a few occasions, but knowing you were out there, waiting patiently, gave me all the impetus I needed to buckle on down and bring the thing to fruition. Book two, has been a hard, convoluted slog, but I'm very happy with the finished result.

All the very best,

KJ

Acknowledgements

Thanks to my lovely editors:

Suzanne Buist
Blossom Young

Also by *K.J.Heritage*

Mystery and Crime
Dying Is Easy
The Peculiar Case of the Missing Mondrian

Science Fiction
Shattered Helix *(Vatic Book 1)*
Shattered Web *(Vatic Book 2)*
Blue Into The Rip
Quick-Kill & The Galactic Secret Service
The Lady In The Glass - 12 Tales Of Death & Dying

Sci-Fi Compilations
Once Upon A Time In Gravity City
Chronicle Worlds: Legacy Fleet
From The Indie Side

Fantasy
The Scowl

Non-Fiction
All About Copywriting: 55 Easy Edits To Improve Your Writing Forever
3000 Writing & Plot Prompts A-C: Supercharge Your Creativity & Improve Your Writing Forever!

Find all ebooks, paperbacks, hardbacks & audiobooks by *K.J.Heritage* at the following stores:

Amazon & Audible, Apple, KOBO, Barnes & Noble/, Nook, Google, Smashwords & more

Links

Join K.J.Heritage's *Newsletter*
Get an inside track on all future releases, access to early
reading copies (ARCs), sneak previews, and more.
http://kjheritage.com/join

Mastodon
@kjheritage@mastodon.online

Instagram
Photos of my wonderful Shollie rescue #RescueJack, piccies
of my best mugs of tea, and various and shameless images
of all my books. Oh and maybe yours truly on a good hair
day!
https://www.instagram.com/k.j.heritage

Twitter:
90K+ followers
@kjheritage

TikTok
General silliness and book stuff. Search for #kjhtok
https://www.tiktok.com/@k.j.heritage

BookBub:
Not only can you check out the latest cool book deals, but
you can also get an alert when I publish my next book
https://www.bookbub.com/authors/k-j-heritage

Goodreads:
Friend me here:
https://www.goodreads.com/kjheritage

K.J.Heritage Facebook Group: *Mostly Readers*
Fun chat and posts about reading… *mostly.*
https://www.facebook.com/groups/mostlyreaders

K.J.Heritage Facebook page: *Mostly Writing*
Follow/like and keep in touch with even more writery stuff!
https://www.facebook.com/mostlywriting/

Website:
http://kjheritage.com/

Email:
Want to get in touch? Well here's your chance
contact@kjheritage.com

About *K.J.Heritage*

"K.J.Heritage's uncanny sense of pacing and
story puts him at the forefront of today's
speculative fiction writers."
**Samuel Peralta, Amazon bestselling author
and creator of The Future Chronicles**

K.J.Heritage writes books that he loves to read. From
science fiction action and adventure mysteries to
contemporary thrillers, comedy, and paranormal fantasy.

When he isn't penning third-person descriptions about
himself, he's an international bestselling author writing
the books he likes to read. From psychological thrillers
and mystery sci-fi to crime, action & adventure, and
epic fantasy. He should really stick to one genre, but he's
not that kind of writer... or reader.

His first sci-fi short story, *Escaping The Cradle* was
runner-up in the 2005 Clarke-Bradbury International
Science Fiction Competition.

K.J.Heritage's short story CHURCHILL'S ROCK,
part of the 'Chronicle Worlds: Legacy Fleet' anthology,
will be aboard the Astrobotic's Peregrine Lunar Lander
set for launch on the United Launch Alliance's Vulcan
Centaur rocket platform bound for the moon in June
2022.

He has also appeared in several anthologies with such

self-publishing sci-fi luminaries as Hugh Howey and Samuel Peralta.

K.J.Heritage has done all the requisite 'writery' jobs such as driver's mate, factory gateman, barman, labourer, telesales operative, sales assistant, warehouseman, IT contractor, Student Union President, university IT helpdesk guy, British Rail signal software designer, premiership football website designer, gigging musician, company director, graphic designer, stand-up comedian, sound engineer, improv artist, magazine editor and web journo... Although he doesn't like to talk about it. *Mostly. Maybe a little bit.*

He was born in the UK in one of the more interesting previous centuries. Originally from Derbyshire, he now lives in the seaside town of Brighton. He is a tea drinker, avid Twitterer, and neurodiverse (ASD) human being.

FOR ALL media enquiries, event/booking information, signed copies, etc. please email: *contact@mostlywriting. com*

All the very best,

K.J.Heritage

www.ingramcontent.com/pod-product-compliance
Lightning Source LLC
Chambersburg PA
CBHW010540170726
48285CB00008B/2692